When

Blood Divides

Linda Jane Martin

K Gerard Martin

Contents

Chapter 1:

Scared

How did this happen? Hiding in an old boathouse because we are being hunted by a mob. They tried to stop our coach on the road. Nathan out-smarted them and has hidden the coach next to this old boathouse.

Lady Antoinette must get her little daughter and ten year old sister out of harm's way. She is getting scared. Her father says everything will calm down once the people get a few good harvests. But she feels the peasants seem too angry and without any hope. She has decided to send her sweet Lily to her English father and Marie to the Covenant of the Holy Mother. After this is all over and under control—she will go fetch them. She wishes she could go with them now, but her mother is too ill.

Lily and Marie are shaking with fear. Lady Antoinette teaches Lily and Marie a song to help calm them from outside agitation. She's hoping they will remember the song when their birthright is restored.

DeBlanche are so Franch
From Valley are Loire

From Main we go May
Then to April not too far.
A rock, a stone, a Shannon Blank tree
Lie hum-bl-y aside the grotto number three.

That is why she finds herself with Lily, Marie, Nursemaid Louise and Henri. The time is now. Lady Antoinette takes off in the coach back to her home with Nathan driving. The angry peasants are chasing her, throwing farming tools and rocks at her coach.

Henri in like kind sneaks Lily, Marie, and Louise into the boat and quietly paddles to a sailboat awaiting departure. For England.

Twelve years later.

Lily, the sixteen-year old daughter of Lord M Hardshore, was strolling along her father's country estate outside of London, England, when she overheard a conversation between two bank associates and her father through the open window.

"Your last venture has fallen through," said one bank associate.

Lord M was taken aback, "I was told that this venture was as good as gold, what happened to the money I gave toward the building of the bridge?"

"As we said the bridge collapsed before it opened and took 75 skilled workers with it—therefore no money was made."

Afraid of what this could mean for her father's estate, she sauntered along toward the estate's entrance as if enjoying the day when in fact she listened with great interest. She would not be disappointed. As the banker associates left the house, Lily heard one banker state to the other that this was the seventh venture that has foundered, and Lord M had better be more careful or all his inherited cash will be lost.

This is what started Lily to question the household financial adviser about how money was made on "ventures". Mr. Carmichael was more than happy to advise his client's daughter, after all she was so sweet with her harmless questions. Only her questions became harder and harder to answer, beginning with the first failed venture, which happened 17 years prior when Lord M resided in London but had made a special visit to Scotland to see a paddle steamer.

Chapter 2:
An Unhappy Wife

Steam arose from Dalswinton Loch on that cool October day the 14th in 1788. Lord M Hardshore, the English aristocrat, and his wife, Colleen, watched the demonstration of a paddle steamer. The water rippled and churned as the steamer glided by. Lord M savored the autumn colors while Colleen boasted the skills of her kinsmen.

"That's Scottish engineering, it is," Colleen declared. "A marvel fit for a king!"

Lord M was not interested. Boats and machines were not meant for each other, he felt. Steam. It much resembled smoke to his mind, like that of a dilapidated axle wheel in need of heavy oil.

"A creature belching clouds upon a loch of beauty belongs not to men of manners and grace," Lord M replied.

Colleen's patience was short. Her Scottish blood held no reservations on the temperament of her tongue.

"It paddles upon water without need for the labor of man," Colleen said. "What excuses should a man now have? No longer can he claim exhaustion as a reason to ignore his wife. Five years ago you made such a promise on the day that we wed. Five years. You have my land and my wealth, and for a family I have the empty steam of a paddleboat."

Nearby dignified folk overheard and moved slowly away as if avoiding a growing plague that might fill them with de-dignification disease. The steam paddler grew closer as did the sounds of its mechanized apparatus. Colleen alternated her facial expression between beaming pride for the paddler stride and disdain for the marital lame.

"Like the beauty of a rose," Colleen said, referring to the paddler.

Lord M checked his gloves for thickness. He turned away from Colleen and looked along the loch's shoreline. A small batch of Scottish thistle caught his attention. With a devilish grin, Lord M snapped off a thistle at the stem and presented it to Colleen.

"A Scottish *rose* for my wife," Lord M said with a-slight affection.

Colleen, trusting her husband to his tender tone, turned and took the plant with eagerness. But her delight turned to pain as the thistle's spines punctured her thin gloves. She threw the thistle down, but her gloves remained embarbed like quills of a porcupine. Enraged, she held out her hands to Lord M with fire in her eyes.

"Remove them!" returned her scathing words.

"This is the flower of Scotland," Lord M replied as he pulled spine after spine from her gloves, though his eyes moved from Colleen to the spines and back as if to muddy his meaning as to Colleen or the thistle being the flower.

"A prickly thistle past its flowering days," Colleen said with eyes glancing at the fallen flora.

"Indeed," Lord M said with cunning eyes toward Colleen.

"How dare you!" Colleen quacked. "Fetch me a doctor!"

Lord M turned away and looked for one of his party. He only saw Carmichael, Lord M's financial adviser, who from a distance was waving his hand toward Lord M with great intent. The two walked toward each other and met halfway.

"Colleen needs a doctor," Lord M said.

"Where is she?" Carmichael asked.

"She is over there," Lord M said with his motion cut short as he realized she was no longer where his memory suggested.

"I do not see her," Carmichael said.

Lord M returned quickly to the tossed thistle. But Colleen was not there. Turning around with speed, Lord M could only see someone speaking briefly but intently with Carmichael before darting away as if with feet on fire. Carmichael strode confidently toward Lord M.

"I cannot find Colleen!" Lord M said with slight anxiety (but only slight).

"Word is she lost patience and departed for her parents in Dalbarth," Carmichael explained, "so that she may receive proper treatment from the family doctor."

"Carmichael, why aren't you in London?" Lord M asked.

"To seek your speedy return," Carmichael said. "I shall explain on the way."

"But Colleen," Lord M started.

"Will be sent word of your departure," Carmichael said. "Hurry, sir."

"I—"

"Hurry!"

Chapter 3:

Departure for France

"My departure?" Lord M said as the two hurried to the inn.

"A pressing business matter awaits you in London," Carmichael said.

A stagecoach was packed and headed back for London with Lord M and Carmichael.

"Explain," Lord M commanded.

The horses kicked up autumn leaves and fallen twigs along the path toward London as the carriage moved along with speed. The carriage occasionally whipped from side to side from uneven earth, striking unfallen branch and shrub. The horses neighed at the crack of the whip.

"Your French creditors have long since called for payment over the failed longbow factory," Carmichael said as a deep rut thrust the two from their seats into the carriage's roof.

"Let them complain. The longbow is a beautiful weapon and deserves to be produced," Lord M said with indifference.

"No one has the patience for mastery of the longbow," Carmichael said. "It is the age of the blasting powder."

"Still, the French are far away," Lord M said with continued indifference.

Another rut, a horse stumbled, and a chunk of dirt flew in through the carriage opening and landed on Lord M.

"The French are hungry and anxious," Carmichael said. "They will not wait. You must sell one of your interests to cover the loss. I have your British portfolio here."

Carmichael handed a packet to Lord M, but Lord M refused.

"I will not sell from this," Lord M said. "Do as I say, Carmichael. Sell nothing from this portfolio. If anything, I will liquidate your services first."

After an hour of silence, the two approached Dumfries.

"We'll stop in Dumfries for a set of fresh horses," Carmichael said. "Must be wary of the emigrants. They might steal from us before they depart for the Americas or Australia."

"Emigrants. Leaving these shores," Lord M mused.

"Yes. Do not become caught up with them."

Lord M grinned.

"Indeed I shall," Lord M said. "And you shall proceed to London without me."

"My Lord?"

"Be I emigrant or passenger, I will give to the French what is French," Lord M said. "I'm going to France."

"But these ships are not going to France," Carmichael said.

"I shall find one. To sell the French vineyard," Lord M said.

"That is not necessary," Carmichael said. "We can arrange all affairs in London."

"Word would get out. I will not have vultures of English aristocracy tear scraps of decency from my flesh," Lord M said. "Besides, I need a French holiday."

Lord M grinned at the thought of a holiday from Colleen and her thistle, even if it meant daring into the country of France.

"Tension is high in France," Carmichael said as the carriage shook over a corduroy part of the path. "Food is scarce. Peasants are hungry and wretched."

"So are my nerves," Lord M said as several leaves covered in spiders and cobwebs flew into the carriage. "Ick!"

"You cannot count on the French aristocracy to protect you. They know not your name," Carmichael said. "They *do* know your wife."

"Yes, Colleen of Dalbarth," Lord M said with a wince.

"She would have to know of your ventures and debt," Carmichael said.

"Not a word!" Lord M insisted. "Send for her to the London home. But that is all!"

Carmichael reluctantly agreed.

On reaching Dumfries, Lord M had Carmichael purchase used clothes from a local. Lord M secretly covered himself in such clothing, carrying a simple bag with his proper clothes and boots, and made way for a boat of emigrants en route for a larger ship in Carsethorn.

Lord M snickered at his game of deception. Pretending to be a desperate commoner with a desire to leave Scotland was an amusing adventure that took his mind off the aristocratic politics that constantly pursued him. His own marriage to Colleen of Dalbarth was just another part of such politics. How he wished to escape things for good and pursue nobler pursuits of old instead of the instant gratification of the nasty blasting powder age that Carmichael reminded Lord M of.

The emigrant boat stopped at Carsethorn, a Scottish town on the Irish Sea. Lord M's shipmates split off to ships of their chosen overseas destinations.

Lord M, however, perused the different ships and inquired as to their destinations, particularly for any bound for France. His inquiries fell upon deaf ears until he stumbled upon a young schooner crew down on their luck. The crew argued as to how they could make reparations for their pirated cargo.

It was the jingling of gold coins that caught their attention. No conversation of length was necessary. Lord M said, "France," jingled his coins, and the crew took Lord M toward France. With the crew eager and Lord M tired, Lord M found himself spending most of his sea voyage asleep or quietly thinking of a place in the country away from the trappings of aristocracy.

Lord M quite lost count of the hours and days, finding himself in the Bay of Biscay on the western shoreline of France. With his instructions being carried out to the letter, the crew sailed to the mouth of the Loire River, where Lord M, who had had enough of the sea adventure, disembarked and took a brief respite at a French tavern where he changed into his proper clothes before hiring a fast coach eastward along the Loire River.

The coach made good its promise of a quick pace, but the journey took all day. Light faded, and so did Lord M's patience. He bade the driver goodbye as he checked himself into an inn for the night.

The next morning, Lord M looked out and realized he was within walking distance of his vineyard.

"I thought the inn familiar," he said to himself.

Anyone else might have walked the distance to the vineyard, but Lord M coerced the innkeeper into calling for a driver to take him to the vineyard guesthouse.

The innkeeper reluctantly agreed.

Chapter 4:

Vineyard and the Lady

Lord M arrived at the vineyard guesthouse, a well-masoned but small building built for special visitors. Carmichael had arranged the purchase, and so this was Lord M's first visit. But Lord M was surprised to find the food stores empty. He called for the caretaker.

"Yes, m'Lord," said the caretaker, who was a disheveled man ravaged by hard work and little food.

"This guesthouse is bare. Where is the food? Why is it neglected? I haven't traveled this way just to see the swindle of my investment," Lord M said.

"I was unprepared for your visit. Begging your pardon, I did not receive word," the caretaker said while shaking in nervous anxiety.

"Inexcusable!" Lord M proclaimed.

"If you will permit me, I shall bring food at once. The missus has baked—"

"Eat servant food? Your insults grow by the moment. Replenish this house with proper stores. Immediately!" Lord M ordered as he threw a small bag of coins at the caretaker.

The caretaker left with the coins as quickly as his tired bones permitted. Meanwhile, Lord M contemplated what else might be awry with his vineyard. Selling without gaining a proper purview could have him fighting disgrace from the French, something he dare not do while in the country.

Lord M ordered his driver to take him across the vineyard. Already, a mad frenzy of harvest was underway, making travel difficult.

"Get out of the way!" Lord M ordered more than once to carts being filled with the harvest.

The crushing of a chance grape here and there filled the air with a pleasant aroma for most, but for Lord M it was a stark reminder of his immediate need for a sale to cover his longbow debt. Several workers happily tossed a grape around to celebrate the harvest, with an errant throw catching Lord M in the eye.

"Vile filth," Lord M shouted at the workers.

The helpers, however, did not understand Lord M's language and simply laughed.

"Hurry onward, driver," Lord M ordered.

But there was really nowhere to go. And so, the driver ended up circumnavigating the property to avoid the hecklesome workers. Lord M had seen enough of the vineyard with its seemingly contemptible workers and was impatient to sell. His nerves were so badly rattled by having to dare so close and thus interact with the workers that he ordered the driver to pause on a hill atwixt his vineyard and another estate.

"What hath my eyes beholden?" he said as his anxiety melted away.

The neighboring estate upon which Lord M cast his eyes was exquisitely architected. It only took seconds for him to recognize it as a French chateau. It looked half-castle and half-mansion, with a beautiful fountain in a courtyard, a well-manicured lawn, and an impressively-colorful flower garden considering the time of year. Lord M forgot all about his troubles (what troubles?) and immersed himself in the beauty of the flower garden, which included ornately decorated statues, benches, little fountains, plenty of paths for leisurely strolls, and an aroma that more than whisked away the fading memory of Lord M's vineyard.

Lord M found himself dismissing the driver the day's remainder while he himself snuck down the hill behind tree and the occasional bramble that bristled past him in an attempt to bring his old life to the forefront. But neither bristle nor bramble could a-sway him from his direction of destiny. For what he now saw bedazzled him far beyond what he could ever prepare himself for.

"A goddess of the garden," he muttered. "A diva divine."

"Il y a quelqu'un?" said a beautiful French woman in a pink and white gown, with ruffles adorning her sleeves and hat. In her right hand she wielded a collapsed parasol like a walking stick.

Lord M decided he could no longer hide like a frightened rabbit. Constrained by his formal attire, he could not return up the hill.

"I am Lord Hardshore, owner of this...vineyard," he started confidently but ended with a doubt on his lips.

The woman laughed.

"An Englishman," she continued to laugh.

"If I may have the honor of your acquaintance," Lord M said, barely able to deliver the words to one of such devilish beauty.

"You do not look like a wayward vineyard worker," she giggled. "I have no need to call the dogs, as you are no longer on your vineyard. Oh, but there is something on your face."

The woman produced a kerchief, walked up to Lord M, and wiped grape remnants from his face. Lord M nearly lost his composure and took her in his arms then and there, but his English stoicism maintained restraint.

"You know English, Princess..." Lord M started, hoping for the woman to reveal her name.

The woman giggled again.

"I am Lady Antoinette," she said. "Lord Hardshore, you are in my garden, or at least the garden of my father's estate, Baron François DeBlanche."

"I've never seen such beauty, Lady Antoinette," Lord M said. "I have traveled all the way from England—"

"To see me? How flattering," she laughed.

"Yes, I mean no, I mean, I came for wine. The vineyard. Oh, I'm not myself," Lord M said.

"Perhaps we should sit on this little bench under shade of tree, though the day is cool enough," Lady Antoinette said.

Lady Antoinette led Lord M to a bench, where the two sat and exchanged glances for several minutes. At length, Lady Antoinette asked about Lord M's journey from England to France. Lord M told the tale, and as he spent more time with the French Lady, his anxiety abated while his new-found friendship grew. At the end of the story, he explained only that he wished to sell the vineyard but not why.

It was Lady Antoinette who mentioned her father's interest in the vineyard, and how it would complement the DeBlanche estate. She would discreetly have word of Lord M's intentions to sell be made known to the DeBlanche financier, and have a messenger be sent to Lord M's vineyard guesthouse. Lord M agreed and thanked the beautiful Lady Antoinette. Lord M made to say, "Farewell," and half-turned to go up the way he came, but Lady Antoinette laughed and showed him another way—a tunnel that led through the hill and toward his guesthouse.

"I am not sure I want to know how or why this tunnel is here," Lord M said.

"Secrecy is of prime importance," Lady Antoinette winked.

Lord M disappeared into the tunnel, traveled its length, and found himself passing through a hidden door in an occupied shed. From there it was only a short walk to the vineyard's guesthouse.

It would have been a short walk. It should have been a short walk. Except for the rabbit hole that caught Lord M's ankle.

Chapter 5:

The Vineyard is Sold

Lord M felt like a hostage in his own guesthouse, carefully hidden in a backroom so as to maintain dignity of his situation. He did what he could to wrap the ankle (his left), but his inflexible nature made such a task difficult. Worse, he could no longer fit his boot over the wrapping. In the end, he removed the wrapping and forced his now swollen foot back into his boot, where it continued to swell until the boot held it firm.

And only just in time. Lord M had but re-entered the main guesthouse area when the messenger arrived as expected.

"Begging your pardon, Lord Hardshore. Baron DeBlanche would be honored with your presence for afternoon tea," the messenger said. "My regrets if you are not Lord—"

"I am Lord Hardshore," Lord M said. "Afternoon tea. Hmm. Like being in London."

"The baron recognizes the fatigue of your long journey and would like to offer his neighborly hospitality," the messenger said. "He has graciously sent his coach to ease the invitation."

The messenger pointed to a lavishly decorated coach with its own driver and horses that waited behind the messenger's lone horse.

"I shall go," Lord M said. "But you will ride behind the coach. No dust from your horse shall cross my brow."

"As you will," the messenger said.

Lord M climbed into the coach, and they were off. The coach took more formal roads as it were (and not the secret tunnel). Lord M winced at the pain in his throbbing ankle, but the boot held firm. When the coach arrived at the DeBlanche estate, he exited the coach and mustered a walking style that hid his injury. Into the estate he entered.

Baron François DeBlanche greeted Lord M and ushered him immediately to the tea room, where servants catered to Lord M's every desire of food and drink. DeBlanche's financier appeared in the doorway, but DeBlanche subtly waved him away.

Lord M thanked DeBlanche for the tea and food, and so Baron DeBlanche ushered them into the smoking room. Both Lord and Baron enjoyed fine pipes and casual discussion. However, Lord M found his foot throbbing and needed to stretch. Baron DeBlanche, not aware of the injury but realizing a bit of walking would be good, suggested the two take a brief walk through the estate.

Upon approach of the music room, Lord M found his heart lifted and ankle pain reduced by the sound of singing. Lord M paused by the doorway to see the singer was Lady Antoinette, accompanied by her lady in waiting on the harp.

"Excuse my manners," Baron DeBlanche said while leading Lord M into the music room. "Lord Hardshore, may I introduce my daughter, Lady Antoinette DeBlanche. Antoinette, this is Lord Hardshore, our neighbor. He is from England."

The pure bliss of Lady Antoinette's beauty overcame Lord M. He stood as if paralyzed by the euphoria (he was). He felt absolutely no pain from his ankle or any agitation from things of his past (or even future). Only that moment of her pure delight mattered.

"A pleasure to meet you, Lord Hardshore," Lady Antoinette smiled with a wink and a shiver of excitement, a reaction that seemed unnoticed by Baron DeBlanche (who we may as well admit was made oblivious by his eager obsession for Lord M's vineyard).

Lord M was too dazed to speak and could only smile in return. Baron DeBlanche ushered Lord M to the baron's office. With Lord M being tranquil from seeing Lady Antoinette, DeBlanche took the opportunity to bring up how much he adored Lord M's vineyard, and if there was anything DeBlanche could do to assist with its upkeep, he was more than happy to offer.

In that short time of Lord M's attention being deprived of Antoinette and focused on the vineyard, the throbbing in his foot returned. It grew by the moment and made clear the pain of his financial situation.

Lord M announced that he would sell to Baron DeBlanche, but added, "As a stipulation of the contract, can you see fit to allow my manager to continue working for the vineyard? He is a very good manager, and his family depends on this living."

The baron was so jubilant that he agreed and called for the financier, who not so coincidentally was just outside the door. He brought forth papers, to which the two signed. When it came to how Lord M should be paid, he asked to arrange that with the financier.

"Excellent," Baron DeBlanche said. "My financier will be happy to make such arrangements. Take all the time you need, and feel free to enjoy the hospitality of my estate. Excuse me if you will."

Baron DeBlanche rushed out to the vineyard to make advanced preparations for running the vineyard under his order. Meanwhile, Lord M, with his ankle in pain nearly beyond his mind, could barely hobble to the financier's office. After Lord M made quiet arrangements for the sale to pay off his French creditors, the financier could no longer hold back his concern for Lord M's foot. The swelling had distorted even his boot.

"Lord Hardshore, if I may recommend the estate doctor," the financier suggested.

A short visit with the doctor could but reduce the pain a little. Though the doctor offered a crutch, Lord M refused. As a further blow while walking through the estate, the music room was now empty, and so was Lord M's heart.

"I'm ready to leave," Lord M said reluctantly. "Make my apologies to Baron DeBlanche."

The financier nodded and made arrangements for the estate coach.

"No," Lord M said. "Call a driver from the inn to meet me in a discreet place. I do not wish to be seen limping away like a mongrel."

The financier sent word for such a driver with instructions on where to pick up Lord M. The financier, however, insisted that Lord M be taken to the location and not be forced to walk on foot. Lord M agreed.

Chapter 6:

A French Farewell

Lord M waited in a grotto, a small cave-like area that had been worked with Roman statues seeming to pour water into a fountain. The grotto kept its cool temperature year-round, and a glance at the empty compartments suggested that it was once used to store food.

A table with two benches neighbored the fountain.

"At least the deal is done," Lord M said to himself as he sat on one of the benches. "I must return to London before anyone suspects anything. For dignity's sake."

Soft steps approached the grotto entrance. Was the driver there already? He best hide behind a pillar.

He did. What he saw required him to clutch his throat. It was Lady Antoinette. What was she doing here? She seemed despondent, as if suffering from sudden loss. Still hidden from view, Lord M watched as she approached the fountain, whispered something, took a cup from a side cupboard, dipped the cup into a fresh stream flowing into the fountain, filled her cup, and paused as she held it to her lips.

Lord M could barely contain himself. The anticipation of watching her drink from the cup nearly overpowered him. Still, he held his position and kept his heavy breathing as quiet as is possible in a grotto.

She took a sip. But just one. She placed the cup on the bench, took one last look of the fountain as if bidding farewell, and left the grotto, resigned and defeated.

Lord M held his position for another moment. But then a carriage drove up, and a driver stood at the grotto's entrance.

"Lord Hardshore? Your driver is here," the driver said.

Lord M wiped his brow in relief. As torn as he was by his feelings, he felt that his English dignity had to be solid. He started out from his hiding place, but before the driver became aware of Lord M's presence, the horse bolted off, and with it a surprised driver running after it.

"I must find a way back to the inn, quietly," Lord M said.

Lord M made for the grotto entrance to find someone, but his nerves were frayed by the bolting horse, and his ankle throbbed again. He had hardly rounded the grotto's entrance to the outside when he bumped into someone with a start.

"Lord Hardshore!" Lady Antoinette exclaimed. "Again I find you hiding like a scared rabbit."

Lord M tried to reposition himself, but his ankle finally gave out, and he collapsed.

"Oh, you are hurt!" she said.

Lady Antoinette attempted to help him stand, he tried holding her off, but in the end he gave in to her charm and allowed her to help him to the bench.

"I have sprained my ankle," he said. "Your doctor was of little help, and so I am—"

"Leaving," she finished. "Without saying goodbye?"

"I am sorry," he said. "I am not myself. If I could but walk, perhaps my mind would clear."

"Let's look at your ankle. Go ahead, take your boot off," she said.

"It is not dignified to—"

"None of that, now. I shall remove it," she said.

Lord M wanted to protest. He should have. This wasn't dignified. But he felt paralyzed by her charm again, and so she attempted to remove his boot. But the swelling prevented it.

"It's no use. I'll have to cut off the boot," he said.

Lady Antoinette laughed.

"Up we go to the fountain," she said as she helped him to his feet. "Sit on the edge and place your foot, boot and all, into the fountain."

"This also is not dignified," he tried to say, but she placed a finger over his lips to quiet him.

"There are healing minerals in the water," she said. "The doctor ignores it, but I find it therapeutic."

The water was cool but not cold, and Lord M felt the poisons of his swollen ankle leech out into the water. The water near his boot was at first dirty from his malaise, but the water flowed and cleaned itself up, leaving Lord M with a slimmed down ankle that easily slid out of his boot. He removed his sock and discovered that his ankle had seemingly healed, with all normal pallor being restored. As Lord M stood up, his previously sprained ankle was fine.

At that moment, the frightened horse returned to the grotto's entrance, but the driver was nowhere to be seen.

"Quick!" Lady Antoinette urged. "Help me with the carriage. Hurry!"

With one hand holding the boot and sock, and the other being pulled along by Lady Antoinette, Lord M found himself running on one boot and a bare foot to the carriage. His ankle held up fine, and he was amazed at how quickly he could move under such circumstances.

Lady Antoinette and Lord M quickly fashioned a dummy from carriage blankets and placed it where the driver might sit. Lady Antoinette took to the driver's seat with the dummy, took the reins, and had the horse suddenly run off in a direction she desired. She quickly handed the reins off to the dummy and jumped off, then walked back to Lord M with a smirk on her face.

"Our little secret," she said back to Lord M.

"Where is the horse going?" Lord M asked.

"In the *other* direction," Lady Antoinette replied.

Lady Antoinette suggested they use the tunnel to get back to his guesthouse without delay so he could rest his foot.

"Ah, that's what you mean by *other* direction," Lord M said. "The horse is a decoy."

The two walked together hand in hand. For the first time, Lord M had no thoughts about his dignity or English pride or reputations—nothing but her. Even the final sight of the distraught driver chasing the horse in the distance as the two entered the tunnel cast no shadow on the moment.

As they arrived at the guesthouse, Lord M invited Lady Antoinette into his library. She tried to help Lord M remove his boot, but Lord M took both her hands and held them close to his chest.

"I feel as I have known you all my life," he said.

Lady Antoinette's eyes shone into his face, and her smile was so lovely he just had to kiss her. He released her hands and enfolded her in an embrace.

Lady Antoinette pressed the palm of her hand on his chest and gave a slight push. Lord M released her immediately and smiled. Lady Antoinette was impressed by his ability to hold himself in check—she could feel the fast beating of his heart, oh what passion.

With a giggle she said, "Meet me at the end of your tunnel tomorrow morning, and we will tour the estate together."

As he breathed, "Yes," she turned and left.

Chapter 7:

Without Reservations

As soon as the sun was up, so was Lord M and racing through the tunnel on foot to meet Lady Antoinette. As soon as he arrived at the entrance, he heard Lady Antoinette say, "What took you so long?"

That wonderful woman was seated on a horse and holding the reins to another horse. With a big smile, she suggested they start their adventure together. Though in the side-saddle position, Lady A released the reins to the other horse and commanded her horse to gallop. Lord M had to jump on his horse with no hesitation to follow, trying to catch up to Lady A.

He was very impressed. Lady A stopped her horse at a very big oak tree. Lord M dismounted and lifted her off her horse. They sat under the tree and spoke of their childhood, growing up, their entry into English and French aristocracy, customs, and cuisine. Lady A also managed to coax Lord M's first name from his lips.

"Mortison," he said. "My classmates teased me with 'Morti'.

"Then I will call you 'Maurice,'" she said.

As the morning waned, Lady A suggested they go to her family's hunting lodge where she had sent her lady in waiting to prepare a lunch.

Lord M said, "Lead on m'Lady."

Arriving at the lodge, they noticed that there was smoke coming out of the chimney. She looked over at Lord M and said, "You had better believe there's a cup of tea for you." With a huge smile, he followed her into the lodge.

In the lodge, they finished their little lunch, she cleaned up their things and packages, they sat with him wrapping his arms around her, and they shared how much they enjoyed each other's company. Lady A turned and placed herself fully upon Lord M's body. She whispered into his mouth:

"I adore you."

...and she kissed him. And that was all the suggestion Lord M needed. He wrapped her face into his two hands, which went around her neck and down her back. When they broke off the kiss, he said:

"I wish to make you mine of passion and wonder."

With a giggle, she started removing her clothes. As her dress fell down, her hair fell down, but not off. He wrapped his hands around her hair, and it was like satin. He quickly removed his clothes and put his body upon hers to further consummate their love.

Shortly thereafter, her lady in waiting arrived to help Lady A resume her respectable façade. As Lady A kissed Lord M goodbye, she said:

"Meet me tomorrow at your tunnel, and we'll continue our adventure."

And she pushed him out the door.

The next day, Lord M got up earlier than before and raced to the tunnel only to have that wonderful woman say, "What has taken you so long?" She threw him the reins of his steed, and with another giggle galloped off, with Lord M following behind.

She takes him to a beautiful pond and tells him this is where she came to swim as a child. Now she doesn't feel at all self-conscious, so she wants him to swim with her in the altogether. Knowing exactly where this will take them, he strips down and jumps in. They swim around each other for a bit, and he is surprised she can swim being a woman. And she says:

"We women can do so many things."

She swims over to him and wraps her body around his. Of which he is shocked, as he doesn't know if he can stand and be able to carry her.

Which he does.

Laying her down by the shoreline, they entwine in the universal kinematics of love. As the sun shines down on them, it warms them. Lady A then suggests they go back to the hunting lodge as a hot cup of tea awaits.

They arrange to make another appointment in two days so that she can attend with her father when he opens his new vineyard. Lord M agrees to meet her at the end of the tunnel in two days.

Two days later, Lord M found Lady A walking toward the tunnel. With his questioning look, Lady A took his hand and led him to the grotto.

"I have something to show you," Lady A said.

She reached for the cup, and turned.

"What?" he said.

Instead of reply, she pulled on the cup holder down, and it made a "click" sound, which opened a door. She pointed toward the opening and said, "This is where

I've been saving the DeBlanche treasure for the future generations as France looks like it is going to tear itself apart."

Lord M took Lady A into his arms and started to dance with her. They looked into each other's eyes with such loving passion, with the water fountain providing the only music they did need. Lord M was so taken with this experience that he wished to preserve it as part of the DeBlanche treasure, as this too was a special treasure to be shared, and so he wrote a little note and placed it amongst the jewels and gems for time and family to honor.

Their passion ran freely unto the next full moon, but Lord M was being called back to London. This was where he told her:

"I don't know if you realize that I'm a married man in England, but I want you to be a part of my life, and I can make you a good home in England with proper staff, comforts, and monthly stipend."

"But I would be your mistress," she said. "And this cannot be. And I cannot leave France as my mother is too ill."

"Then this will have to be good-bye for now," he said. "This will not be good-bye forever. I really don't want to leave you. I will try to finish my urgent business affairs and return to your arms."

So they hugged and kissed and cried.

Chapter 8:

Letters from France

Life in London for Lord M was rather benign as his estate entered 1789. His debts were clear, his next business venture was on the horizon, and Colleen for the most part kept to her own affairs. Despite efforts to start a family with her, Colleen never conceived. Periodically, she reminded Lord M that he was at fault for their childless marriage, and she suggested all sorts of wild spices be placed in his food, but such spices would only inflame his throat, resulting in an occasional extra drink to balance the equation.

One day in late April, as thoughts of spring flowers enchanted Lord M's mind for the first time in his life, his financial adviser, Mr. Carmichael, brought a letter to Lord M's attention.

"My Lord, I have a note of gratitude from Baron DeBlanche regarding the vineyard sale. He is happy to report that despite the poor harvest suffered by other Frenchmen, the vineyard has survived the winter unscathed," Carmichael said.

"Excellent," Lord M said. "I should be ready for my next financial venture."

"There is also another note by a feminine hand, addressed to you," Carmichael said, handing Lord M an envelope with a wax seal.

Lord M broke the seal and read the note. Several expressions crossed his face, first one of surprise, then of glee, then a smirk as if planning revenge.

"My Lord?" Carmichael said.

"Here. Read it yourself," Lord M said boldly as he passed the note to Carmichael.

Carmichael started reading the note. Shock crossed his eyes.

"The baron's daughter?" Carmichael said.

"Are you questioning me?" Lord M returned. "I *am* a man."

Carmichael read more.

"Say it, Carmichael," Lord M said.

"I dare not," Carmichael said. "I should not be reading this at all."

"But you are. Per my orders. Lady Antoinette is expecting a child," Lord M grinned.

"My Lord, this—"

"Do you know what this means?" Lord M continued. "I'm not the problem, Colleen is. She's as barren as a frozen desert. I knew it. I knew it!"

Carmichael shook his head in disbelief and said, "We must burn the letter before Lady Colleen—"

"Reseal the letter," Lord M said. "Mix it in with her arriving letters. See if she takes notice."

"I cannot. I will not!" Carmichael said as he dropped the note on his desk.

"Then your employment ends," Lord M said.

Carmichael grimaced, twisted a cloth, and wiped it across his sweaty brow. He opened his mouth to voice concern, but he needed his job, and so the mouth closed.

"There. It's all settled," Lord M grinned.

The discovery of the note by Colleen from Lady A to Lord M did not have the effect on Colleen Lord M desired. She became less vocal about her complaints in general, and she never directly brought up the visit to France nor the affair Lord M had had with Lady A. Lord M in turn never brought it up, and this became a waiting game, to see who would bring it up first.

Neither did, but strange things happened at Lord M's estate. First, conversations became flat, more ordinary, and about day-to-day minutia. Second, Lord M never saw the full letter from Lady A again. Instead, bits and pieces of it would mysteriously appear in various places. Several times it appeared in his afternoon tea without any explanation from the servants. Other pieces would show up in his food as he bit into it. Colleen would listen but not look during these moments, waiting for Lord M to complain about the torn pieces. He did not.

It didn't matter what he did on the estate nor how seemingly private, another piece would show up. Just the fact that these pieces would show up in places Lord M considered secret put him on edge. When would his Scottish wife go into full volcanic rage?

Early July of 1789, and another letter arrived from Lady Antoinette to Lord M. Lord M read it quietly and then ordered Carmichael to read it.

"Must I, my Lord?" Carmichael asked before being given the look. "Very well. Lady Antoinette wishes you well, that she expects to have her child soon. She is in Paris with her father on political business. Paris is beautiful. She is thankful for the child she is about to bear and asks nothing in return. The child will bring her much joy and remind her of the wonderful time you two had together. There is more, but it's written in French. Appears to be French poetry."

Lord M grinned again then stated, "To poetry goes poetry."

"My Lord?"

"That book Colleen drools over," Lord M started. "By that Scottish poet."

"By Robert Burns," Carmichael said. *"Poems, Chiefly in the Scottish Dialect."*

"With the engraving in the front," Lord M said.

"An engraving of Robert Burns himself," Carmichael said.

"Paste the letter atop the engraving," Lord M said.

"I would not dare intrude upon—"

"Make the paste from flour and water," Lord M continued. "So that bread from Heaven may grow from this flour."

"It is likely to mold," Carmichael said.

"Do it," Lord M said, and he left Carmichael with the note.

"Will this count as a failed venture?" Carmichael asked himself. "It has all the markings of one. Dear me. Lady Colleen will surely lose her temper over this one."

But Colleen did not. She did find the note, yes, but again Lord M missed his mark. Instead, he began discovering bits and pieces of the Burns poetry book in his food, his drink, and all the other places that pieces of the earlier letter were placed. Even when he took to the estate bathhouse, he found bits of Burns poetry floating by. But nowhere did he find bits of the second letter.

The effect on Lord M was one of conquest. Bits of a Scottish book here and there were not incriminating evidence, and so he felt confident his adventure in France was well-justified. What book would Colleen tear up next? It didn't matter. She was reacting, and that was all Lord M could hope for.

Late July of 1789. Lord M approached Carmichael, holding a copy of the London Gazette for July 18th to July 21st.

"Have you seen this?" Lord M said, pointing to a section of the newspaper missing.

"I'll send for another copy," Carmichael said as he signaled to one of the servants.

"Colleen and her mischief," Lord M grinned.

A servant brought another copy of the Gazette in and handed it to Carmichael. Lord M, however, was too engrossed with his plans to notice immediately. Carmichael, who had trained himself to half-listen, was already reading through the Gazette's missing section using the good copy.

"My Lord, a body of troops entered Paris. Two dragoons were killed. Oh, this goes on. Consternation. A detachment went to the Bastille. The Governor ordered the guard to fire. Several killed. A detachment of forty passed the drawbridge. All massacred. It says, 'This Breach of Faith, aggravated by so glaring an Instance of Inhumanity, naturally excited a Spirit of Revenge and Tumult not to be appeased.'"

Lord M took the good copy and read with intent.

"Antoinette," he whispered under his breath. "Have there been any letters from Paris? Any letters from *her*?"

"None," Carmichael said.

"This could be quite the interesting situation," Lord M mused. "France is unsteady, and a French son of mine could one day take advantage of that unrest and take leadership. Why, he could acquire French property and wealth far beyond what I have accomplished in England. A tribute to his heritage. Yes, a proud son I will soon have. We could then bring some sort of peace between our countries. Unite them. Why, I could lay challenge to the King of England and his scions. He's not fit to rule!"

Carmichael dismissed any servants within earshot.

"Why did you do that? I'm Lord here," Lord M said.

"To save your dignity," Carmichael said. "I will not be silent. You sound as off-keel as King George himself."

"I will not be spoken to that way, Carmichael. Your employment will become more fragile by the day with such talk. Keep to the finances. That is what you do best."

"You have had me do other things besides that," Carmichael said.

"Yes. I have one more thing for you to do," Lord M said. "Those words you read from the Gazette—about Breach of Faith—place them on a plaque in the main courtyard."

"Those are words about the French," Carmichael said. "They do not apply to England. People will not understand."

"Colleen will. She took my piece of the paper, after all," Lord M said.

Carmichael reluctantly agreed. And so, the plaque was posted:

This *Breach* of *Faith*
Aggravated by so glaring
An *Instance* of *Inhumanity*
Naturally excited
A Spirit of *Revenge*
And *Tumult*
Not to be appeased

Lord M half-expected the plaque to be torn up into bits and placed into his food and drink. Or at least parts of the Gazette distributed in like fashion. But none of this happened. However, Lady Colleen did make additional trips to her family in Dalbarth, with no explanation, only for a few days at a time, and returning as if nothing were amiss.

In early August of 1789, Lord M received a letter from Lady Antoinette. Wanting to brag of his French association, he had Carmichael read it first.

"Lady A is safe," Carmichael said to a pleased Lord M. "She was, however, in Paris during the Bastille violence. She was giving birth to your child. Friends helped her escape to the summer home. It was not easy. She bled heavily during the journey."

"What did she name my son?" Lord M pressed. "What name did she give to the future King of France?"

"Lily Marie Hardshore."

Lord M's pallor failed him. His jaw dropped, and his spirits sank.

"You have a daughter," Carmichael said calmly.

Lord M paced back and forth. Then in circles. He lit a pipe and drew from it heavily.

"There's still time for another venture," Lord M said. "I shall go to France and find another Antoinette."

"What?" Carmichael asked in disbelief.

"Do not question my word. I am the Lord Hardshore," Lord M said. "I shan't be gone long."

With much speed, Lord M had his things packed, took a carriage to port, and sailed on the quickest ship to the mouth of the Loire River in France. He immediately disembarked the ship and took to a land route as before, but the way was slow and treacherous.

Expecting to receive noble courtesy from the peasants, Lord M instead was nearly constantly under assault. It was the tail end of the Great Fear, when peasants attacked nobility from lack of food. Lord M nearly lost his life two times, and after the third, he returned to London without any romantic conquests.

"Another failed venture," Carmichael half asked, half stated.

"It was not the same France," Lord M said. "A pity, really. Well, I must get on with things. Hone in on business at home."

"Honing in at home" for Lord M meant spending his money loosely with loose company in London. At least overseas travel was spared.

Lady Colleen immersed herself in charity work with other Ladies. There were other things she did aside of Lord M, of which Lord M had no knowledge or interest.

In late July of 1790, Lord M received a letter from Lady Antoinette that Lily had celebrated one year of age on July 14th. The celebration coincided with the Fall of Bastille celebration. Lady Antoinette, however, made it a point that Lily's celebration had to be kept private and away from the Bastille celebration, as the nobility were still fearful of the French unrest.

"I must give thought to an overseas venture," Lord M said to Carmichael. "No, not France. I must think beyond small-ish countries like France."

"France a small country?" Carmichael said in surprise.

"Yes," Lord M said. "Great land commands great food. Grapes are too small."

"Too small?" Carmichael asked.

"Do not interrupt," Lord M said. "What does England need right now? I have the answer. Fruits, that's the secret, Carmichael. Fruits as large as a loaf of bread. Or larger. Grown in a large land, untouched by all this European squabbling. New England. That's the place where I shall make my next fortune."

"My Lord, that was already tried," Carmichael said. "It did not—"

"It will be a new cash crop," Lord M said. "All it needs is my vitality and charming veneer. I can charm a French Lady; I can charm a new nation."

Lord M left for the Americas to supervise his new business venture. Carmichael stayed behind and took on increasing responsibility for the estate. Carmichael (reluctantly) at times made excuses for Lord M, suggesting that Lord M was away somewhere in England on a business trip, and so Carmichael signed for Lord M as if nothing were amiss.

Late July of 1791, and coincidentally Carmichael received two letters from abroad. One was from Lady Antoinette telling of Lily's two-year birthday celebration and the continued evasion from peasant persecution. The other was from Lord M telling of "setbacks" in getting fruit to grow. He did mention a way of growing oranges the size of grapes inside a building. He had hopes he could get them to grow larger.

During Lord M's visit to the Americas, Colleen held numerous gatherings at Lord M's London estate, hosting all the local aristocracy. The meetings, though casual and furnished with food and drink, had an underlying serious tone, and the British landowners were very concerned with the unrest in France. Plans were made to support one another from a possible French invasion. The protection of Great Britain was paramount.

In late July of 1792, Carmichael again received two letters from abroad. A letter from Lord M told of his experiments with cutting seeds and fruit in half to see if they'd double their output. A letter from Lady Antoinette told of Lily's third birthday celebrated in secret, as the DeBlanche family was fearful of an instrument being used with more frequency, the *louisette*, proposed by physician Doctor Guillotin as a humane method of execution.

The anxiety Carmichael felt in reading Lady A's letter caused him to inadvertently cut his hand with the letter opener as he attempted to open other arriving documents. He looked at his bloodied hand and spoke:

"Blood from an instrument meant to free the words of people, or silence them."

October of 1792 produced a letter from Lord M, who lamented further setbacks with the fruit farms. He planned to slice plants in multiple places to expedite growth enhancement for the spring. Carmichael, who overheard much about tension between France and Great Britain from Colleen's noble gatherings, decided it time to send for Lord M's return, fearing for his safety. And so, a note was sent across to the Americas.

Late January of 1793 produced a letter from Lady Antoinette. She had not been told of Lord M's departure for the Americas. As a point in fact, Carmichael put up the pretense of Lord M being at his London estate, and so that kept Lady A somewhat at ease, at least over Lord M's fortunes. She wished to see him but was afraid to travel at all, especially now that King Louis XVI had been beheaded. Lady A was proud of Lily and was sure Lord M would be proud of her too.

France declared war on Britain in February of 1793. No word from Lord M or Lady A.

In March, rumors swirled in the Hardshore estate that a ship from the Americas to England had been captured by a French ship. Colleen suspected Lord M was aboard and pushed her fellow aristocrats to secure the American ship's rescue. After a short engagement (and with no loss of British life), British ships secured the American ship's freedom. The American ship was cheered on its arrival in port, and aboard was, yes, Lord M. Colleen and Carmichael were there at the port to welcome him. Colleen, with a sudden heart of forgiveness, gave him an embrace and a kiss.

"Such a welcome!" Lord M said. "I am glad to return my tired feet to Great Britain."

"Great Britain!" the people cheered.

Colleen escorted Lord M back to the estate. Meanwhile, Carmichael took count of Lord M's American losses after much discussion with the ship's captain.

"An expensive venture," Carmichael muttered to himself.

Spring and summer of 1793 at the Hardshore estate saw Lord M and Colleen in partnership assisting the British effort in the war against France. This new sense of relationship brought them closer, and they celebrated each day with a meal toasting Great Britain. So strong was this work relationship that Carmichael could hardly believe himself. So often had Lord M failed with ventures before, but this one actually brought finances into the estate, enough to cover past losses and build a little extra for comfort. It was hardly believable, and each day Carmichael waited for the other shoe to drop, but it did not.

And so, in mid-September, a letter from Lady A arrived. Carmichael, not wanting to jinx the current good luck at the Hardshore estate, read the note privately without notice to anyone else. Lady A wrote that this would most likely be her last letter, that tension in France was unbelievably high, and given the state of war between France and Britain, she could not risk another letter lest she be painted a traitor and be executed. In her heart, she wished the two countries could be at peace, so that she could see Lord M again. But as it was, this was farewell.

Carmichael burned the letter. It had to be done, as a proper business ending to a "failed venture" that "should have failed off completely". His burning of the letter would make it so.

"Fortunately," Carmichael said to himself, "she ended it. Words from France need not tread upon this estate again."

Chapter 9:

Flight to Safety

It was a beautiful October 1793 day in London, England. The Hardshore estate played host to the wedding of Colleen's niece, Amelia Dalbarth, and Amelia's fiancé, Edward Moore. The wedding being spectacular and of much celebrated happiness, the wedding party and in fact all invited took comfort in the splendid outdoor reception extravaganza. Food, drink, and dance became the order of the day, and all were merry. Many of noble ilk congratulated.

Wagons of supplies poured in throughout the day, and so it was of little notice when a wagon with a man, a woman, and a four-year old child entered the estate. Carmichael, the only unhappy person of the day (because of the event's expense), took to review the cost of each wagon of supplies as it arrived, fueling his craving to cringe at every unnecessary expenditure. And so it was when he pulled aside the wagon with the four-year old child.

"You are not part of the provisions," Carmichael said. "State your business."

"*Excusez-moi, s'il vous plaît.* We are from France. I am Henri, the head servant of the DeBlanche family. We have come to see Lord Hardshore," said the man.

A shadow of dread drained the lifeblood from Carmichael's pallor, and he felt his stomach drop to the underside of his feet, as if the most devastating business venture had placed itself before his path.

"Pull aside," Carmichael said.

Carmichael led the wagon to a side shed used for storing gardening supplies. It was unused at the moment, as the gardening crew had been given the day off to keep clear of the celebration.

"DeBlanche family," Carmichael said.

"Yes," Henri said. "We were sent here by the DeBlanche family."

"For employment?" Carmichael asked. "What sort of work do you do?"

"Nothing of the kind," Henri said. "We cannot stay and must return to France."

"Then why are you here?" Carmichael asked.

"I am Louise, the nursemaid," the woman said. "We are here to give safety to this child."

"I'm sorry," Carmichael said. "But we do not employ children. Such a child as this should be with her parents."

"That is why we are here," Henri said. "This is Lily, daughter of Lord Hardshore."

Carmichael gasped and nearly bit his thumb as he attempted to cover his mouth.

"But...this was not expected. Lily should be with her mother, with Lady Antoinette," Carmichael said.

"Baron DeBlanche terminated the employment of all vineyard workers in violation of the agreement made with Lord Hardshore," Henri said. "The workers retaliated and have vowed to kill anyone of DeBlanche blood. Lily was in mortal danger."

"She has nowhere else to go," Louise said.

"Here are her papers," Henri said, handing papers to Carmichael.

"This is completely out of order," Carmichael said as he placed the papers inside his vest.

Noises from distantly outside the shed approached. Henri peered through a crack in the wall.

"British sentries," Henri said.

"They will take us captive," Louise said.

"Please," Henri said. "Give us a diversion to escape."

"Please!" Louise pleaded.

Carmichael, who looked all around in bewilderment, finally exited the shed and directed the sentries elsewhere. Carmichael then turned about in time to see Henri's and Louise's wagon leave the shed and thus the estate.

"I hope the shed is empty," Carmichael muttered to himself.

But a quick check revealed that Lily had remained behind and had made herself comfortable in a chair. The shed was not inhospitable. It contained a water pump, a small cot, dried fruit, and took from the earth its temperate ambiance.

"Do not leave this shed," Carmichael said.

Lily smiled, like a child with her own playhouse. Meanwhile, Carmichael buzzed about the estate in a frantic fit, looking hither and thither for someone to salvage the scenario.

After several moments, matters of estate finances stole his attention, and soon the thoughts of Lily's presence fell by the way. As the afternoon waned, less common acquaintances of the party departed, leaving but just a core group of close family and nobility.

The group then moved inside to the estate's great hall, which was set up with decorations, more food and drink, and a musician balcony to the side where musicians played soft, happy melodies of congratulations and cheer.

Colleen led Amelia and the group to the other end of the hallway, where a large cloth decorated with the Dalbarth family coat of arms was suspended in front of a small raised platform known as a dais.

"I have a special gift for you," Colleen said to Amelia. "Exquisitely decorated with our family emblems. I want you to feel proud when you have that special guest or simply wish to pass the afternoon in thoughtful reflection and leisure."

The cloth was lifted from the dais, revealing an ornately crafted golden chair fit for a queen's throne. But surprisingly enough, someone was sitting in it.

"Why it's a girl," Amelia said.

"She is not included," Colleen said with a general laugh from the group.

"What is your name?" Amelia asked the little girl.

But before the girl answered, a sudden chill overcame Colleen. The girl somehow reminded her of Lord M. Colleen looked back toward Lord M, who only shrugged his shoulders, not understanding what she meant.

"Lily," the girl said with a French accent.

Colleen pulled Amelia back as horror set in. A French girl sat on a Scottish throne meant as a gift from one Scottish Lady to another. A French girl. A French girl that resembled Lord M.

"Carmichael!" Colleen yelled.

Carmichael, who had been in the very back of the group (since he wasn't actually part of the nobility), pushed his way through with a new anxiety as if a Pandora's box had been opened. As Carmichael caught glimpse of Lily (yes, the same girl he'd seen in the shed), he quickly ushered Lord M and Lily to a back room.

"What is the meaning of this?" Lord M asked. "I am Lord M. You are not to rush me in such fashion."

"Yes, you are Lord M," Carmichael said. "And this is your daughter, Lily."

Colleen entered the room in time to hear Carmichael's last words. The fury of the known universe could not compare to Colleen's outburst. She threw breakables in all directions, including several over Lord M's head and a couple toward Lily, shouted Scottish of the most unpleasant nature at the top of her lungs, spat at Lord M, spat at Lily, shouted further epithets, ripped at Lord M's clothing, coughed up her guttural utterings onto Lord M's face, and kicked him multiple times.

Lord M fell to the floor. Several servants had heard the event, came to see, and quickly went into damage-control mode by ushering guests as far away as possible and having the musicians play at their loudest.

"No claim of Scotland shall the French make over me!" Colleen shouted, in the only words of English she spoke the rest of the day.

Colleen left. Lily broke into soft tears and hid behind a chair. Carmichael helped Lord M to another chair and made him a strong drink. A servant came in and quietly whispered the word that the party was over, and guests departed for home.

The estate was eerily quiet. Colleen had departed shortly after the guests, Lily had stopped crying and instead fell asleep, and both Carmichael and Lord M had finished their drinks. The nearby ticking of a grandfather clock was the only evidence that time itself had not stopped.

But time *had* stopped for Lord M. He fidgeted with a nearby copy of the London Gazette. Lily awoke, and she herself fidgeted with a piece of paper concealed in her clothing. She crawled out from behind the chair and handed it to Lord M.

"So this is Lily," Lord M said. "How did you get here?"

Lily pointed at Carmichael, and said, "He knows."

"Carmichael?" Lord M said.

Carmichael produced a set of papers and handed them to Lord M, the same set of papers passed to him from Henri.

"You should not have allowed this, Carmichael," Lord M said. "I'm holding you responsible."

"She is your daughter, my Lord," Carmichael said.

"She should be in France," Lord M said. "With her mother. This is no place for her."

"France is ripping apart at the seams," Carmichael said. "It is no place for a child."

Lord M paused, lit a pipe, and took several puffs.

"This ends everything. Everything! Do you hear?" Lord M said. "My image is ruined."

"Give Colleen time to regather herself," Carmichael said. "You may yet salvage things with her."

"I was referring to my image among nobility," Lord M said. "Colleen is well beyond my reach by now."

Another pause transpired. Then Lily recited the song her mother taught her:

> *DeBlanche are so Franch*
> *From Valley are Loire*
> *From Main we go May*
> *Then to April not too far.*
> *A rock, a stone, a Shannon Blank tree*
> *Lie hum-bl-y aside the grotto number three.*

Carmichael smiled, but Lord M returned a grim expression.

"I will move to the country," Lord M said.

"And Lily?" Carmichael asked.

Lord M gave a stare to Lily, not one of love, but one of remorse.

"And Lily," Lord M finally mustered.

Chapter 10:

The Search for Lady A

Following the arrival of Lily from France, Colleen returned to her landstake in Scotland. Shortly thereafter, the marriage to Lord M was annulled. With estate ownership matters settled, Lord M moved to the country as desired to preserve his dignity (and sanity). Carmichael, Lily, and a handful of servants loyal to Lord M moved with him.

However, Carmichael pointed out it was improper for Lily to be without a maternal family figure, and so Lord M's mother also moved to the country estate for such purpose.

Lord M sent word to the DeBlanche family, demanding that Lily be taken back since Lily was born in France and thus French. But not long after sending the message, it was returned with a note that no messages could be sent to the DeBlanche family.

Lord M felt saddled with Lily. He paid her little attention and allowed his mother to handle most of Lily's affairs. However, Lord M's mother also felt saddled with Lily. She had only moved in with Lord M until Lily could return to France.

"Had this been a boy of British blue blood," Lord M's mother would say, "that would be different. He could go into business proper-like and add to the family fortune."

Lord M paced back and forth in Carmichael's office.

"I must find the DeBlanche family. I must go to France and make arrangements for Lily's return," Lord M said.

"You can't!" Carmichael said. "There's a war on with France. Did you forget?"

"I could save some effort and take Lily with me. Take her directly to the DeBlanche estate," Lord M continued.

"Lord M. Up to this point, I have been patient with your failures. So far, they have cost only money. Nothing more. But what you propose will get you both killed. It is suicide! I will do everything in my power to stop you!" Carmichael said.

"I can't live like this, Carmichael," Lord M said.

"You have distanced yourself from the London aristocracy. Your finances are stable. Your mother is here, and so is your daughter. What is the crisis?" Carmichael said.

"Either I return Lily to France and take a new wife for a new family," Lord M started.

"Or?" Carmichael added.

"Or I make Lady Antoinette my new wife," Lord M stated.

Carmichael looked outside his office door and instructed nearby staff to shoo the others and themselves away. He then closed and locked his office door.

"We've been through this," Carmichael said. "You can't take Lily back to France. You can't stay in France. As a British citizen, you'd be executed as the enemy."

"That is not of what I speak," Lord M said. "Lily would stay here. I would bring Lady Antoinette here."

"No British ship will take you there. No French ship is allowed in a British port to fetch you, and if they could, they would execute you as a British spy once you reached French waters. No," Carmichael said.

"Then I'll go as an American of Boston, Massachusetts, United States of America," Lord M said with a stretched American accent.

Carmichael looked at Lord M in bewilderment.

"I picked up the accent when I was over there," Lord M said with his usual English accent. "America is neutral in this war with France. In fact, I could pose as an American, sympathetic to the French cause."

"You would still need transportation," Carmichael said.

"You have connections, Carmichael. Find me an American ship and hire it for transport to France," Lord M said.

Carmichael tapped his fingers on his desk in nervous thought.

"Even as an American, you won't know the native language," Carmichael said. "Word is the French are not so sympathetic to speakers of English, even if American, unless they are willing to speak French themselves."

"A minor technicality," Lord M said. "Find me passage, and find me a French guide."

"You will owe me mightily after this venture, *if* you return alive," Carmichael said.

"I shall pack my things," Lord M said.

Carmichael sent a subordinate to make inquires for an American ship and a French guide for the trip. But the subordinate returned with great concern. He voiced these concerns to Carmichael who in turn pondered them before reporting to Lord M.

"I must tell you the circumstances of things," Carmichael finally said in a meeting with Lord M. "There is exactly one French guide willing to take you to France, but no American ships. The French guide has his own ship."

"Well done. I am ready to go," Lord M said.

"Wait. Hear me out. The French guide is Damien DeVille. He is a merchant of goods. And slaves," Carmichael said.

"How do I meet him?" Lord M asked.

"Did you hear me? Slaves!" Carmichael said. "He smuggles slaves out of France to an English port, where an American ship takes the slaves to America. For profit."

Lord M seemed impatient.

"We have never dealt with his kind," Carmichael said. "It's unconscionable."

"I will meet with him and decide for myself," Lord M said.

Carmichael gave Lord M directions for the nearby pub. Lord M went. It was a run-down pub with walls, tables, and floors that reeked of foul bargains and men. Lord M stood out by his proper dress and mannerisms, so much so that the patrons became suspicious. Finally, the pub owner asked if he was lost.

"No," Lord M said. "I am looking for a man. A Mr. DeVille, Damien DeVille."

"There is no one here for you," the owner said.

Lord M placed several gold coins in the owner's hand.

"Not at any price," the owner said.

"Are you certain?" Lord M asked.

"I am certain," the owner replied. "You might find proper food on the other side of town."

Lord M was puzzled. He was in the pub where Damien DeVille supposedly made his dirty deals. But what could he do? He looked around, hoping one of the patrons would wave him over with a friendly smile, but all he got were grim stares.

"Carmichael's wild-goose chase to divert me," Lord M muttered to himself. "He shall hear about this."

Lord M left the pub. He walked past an alley, felt a blow to the head, and blacked out. When he came to, he found himself in a small, dingy room sitting in a chair with several old tallow candles burning on a small table to the side. The stench of the tallow was like that of rotten grease, and he felt sick to his stomach. It was all he could do to hold his gut from retching, and he gagged on the thick candle smoke.

"Mortison Hardshore," a voice with a thick-French accent said.

"I am Lord M, yes," Lord M replied with a suffering throat. "Please address me by my title."

The voice and several others laughed.

"That could get you killed," the voice said.

"Who are you?" Lord M asked.

"I am Damien DeVille," the voice said. "With me are my compatriots. Your financier arranged this meeting."

"I find it disconcerting that Carmichael arranged my meeting in this fashion with injury endured," Lord M said, rubbing the injured part of his skull.

"Yes, most unfortunate that we found you like that," Damien DeVille said, though something in his voice suggested that he was behind the clubbing. "However, times call for a guarded approach. And guarded travels. It is said you wish to visit France. I can help you with that, but you choose an awkward time to visit. For that, the price will be high."

"I am prepared to pay you with gold coins," Lord M said.

Damien chuckled.

"In France, death punishes those who hoard riches of any kind—the noble and their halls of riches, the clergy and their churches of gold, and anyone who hoards wealth of any kind. No, Mortison, I will only accept payment of a more permanent kind, in a country with stability," Damien said.

"What then?" Lord M asked.

"I will tell you. But first, listen. I will take you to France. But you cannot go as nobility. Nor can you go as an Englishman. No, you must be a simple commoner from America. And to be that commoner, you must yield something you acquired while there," Damien said.

"I acquired nothing but a failed orange crop," Lord M said.

"You won three slaves in a gambling game while in America," Damien said while holding three documents of purchase.

"I know nothing of this," Lord M said.

"You were drunk, you bet heavily in a game of cards, and did not know what your opponent threw into the wager. You passed out as your hand was revealed," Damien said.

"Stories," Lord M said. "Why tell stories when I seek passage to France?"

"They are no stories," Damien said. "One of my operatives was watching you and passed himself off as your aide, taking the documents on your behalf, bringing them back to me as a wedge of negotiation if ever needed. I cannot use them as is, as they bear your name of ownership. And so, I will have you sign them over to me."

"Slavery," Lord M said. "I cannot believe I am part of such misery."

"But you are. Sign them to me," Damien said.

An assistant handed several folded documents to Lord M. He began signing them over. But after signing the third document, he reached an unexpected fourth document.

"This isn't for a slave," Lord M said. "It's a landstake."

"In England, yes. A piece of land in London that you have apparently forgotten," Damien said.

"I ordered Carmichael to sell all land in London," Lord M said in anger.

"He did not know. This belonged to your grandmother, who left it in a secret trust until you sired a son," Damien said.

"Don't use such language with me!" Lord M snapped.

An assistant cracked his whip across Lord M's face.

"Don't lose your wit!" Damien snapped back. "Sign over the landstake to me. Quickly. Or no France!"

Lord M signed the landstake to Damien.

"Wisdom does occasion you on this moment," Damien said. "It occasions us all from time to time, but often in strange ways. France persecutes its nobility, and from this a man's senses become acute, sensing the faint traces of nobility and its effect in all its manifestations. He first learns this for self-preservation, later for self-confidence, and later still for self-serving ventures. One might say the Revolution of France has created my thirst for acquisition, honed it, and made me its scion. Come then. Let me show you my homeland, the place that made me."

Damien DeVille and his company took Lord M aboard a small fishing vessel with a minimum of amenities, so as to give Lord M a gruff appearance. Damien introduced him as "Hardy" to the crew and cautioned Lord M to use such name in their French journey.

The French journey commenced. Lord M performed menial labors on the fishing boat to convince the passing ships of his and his crewmates' lack of nobility, lack of religion, and lack of hoarding. Those ships that did more than simply pass, in other words, who intercepted and boarded the fishing boat to satisfy suspicion were instead treated to a meal of rotting fish and moldy bread. After such a meal, the passing ships were quick to leave Damien's boat to shed their stomachs of such vileness.

Lord M wasn't sure how much more he could endure. He had become sick himself, but the ship herbal master put something in Lord M's bread, and it was enough to hold Lord M together. He was still miserable, but at least he was able to hold his stomach together.

"Lady A," he said to himself. "I hold you in my heart, that we may soon be together again."

It was a stormy day in October of 1793 when Damien's fishing boat reached the mouth of the Loire River. Damien and his crew spoke French and convinced the suspicious French people that they were not nobility, were not clergy, and did not hoard anything of value. Damien plied Lord M with alcohol to soften the misery of France, and so Lord M was introduced as the babbling drunk American who claimed to grow oranges in the snow-covered mountains of New England and was looking for beer made from oranges.

Lord M, despite his haze, requested that Damien guide him into deeper France. But Damien laughed.

"I will send one of your former slaves as your guide," Damien said. "She speaks French as well as anyone, in addition to English."

Damien gave out a call, and an older woman showed up with a heavily scarred face. One eyelid was completely closed over in scars while the other was barely open.

"Joie, this is Hardy. Hardy, meet Joie."

Joy. It was hardly a fitting name for this wretch of a woman. Lord M wasn't sure if he should be thankful or reviled.

"She grew up in France with great aspirations for a life in the New World," Damien explained. "She sold herself passage across the Atlantic as an indentured servant. Her master in the New World had, shall we say, a poor sense of judgement for most things, including how to treat people."

"Why aren't you coming with me, Damien?" Lord M asked. "Haven't I paid enough?"

"You have, but France doesn't recognize such payment," Damien said. "I am no fool. I will not risk my neck to any falling blade of steel while in France. You and Joie may take that risk. She knows the country well enough to take you anywhere. She is on loan. I expect her return upon your own as payment for passage back to England. I shall wait one week. Ten days at the most. After that, well, war is just another business deal upon the next day. I will be onto matters of more import."

Lord M agreed. The two made the journey toward his old vineyard. Joie wasn't much for speaking, but she did groan every now and then from the pain in her joints. Lord M had not been provided with alcohol for the trip, and so he took on an exceedingly strong headache from the hangover. Worse, the French people's misery carried over and added to his own. No matter what community he tried to avoid, the story was the same. People of means, of religion, or of other suspicion were executed by what someday would be called the guillotine. Lord M cringed at the sight of dogs lapping up blood from the recently severed heads, but Joie seemed immune to the horror, as if it were not hideous enough to displace that which she had experienced in her own life of servitude.

Many times were the two interrogated as to their business. Joie explained that Hardy (Lord M) was looking to grow oranges for making beer. Most ignored them after that. Some, however, took pity on Joie and asked her to join the Revolution, especially if she could get help from the Americans with Hardy's help. But Lord M played into this by acting like a drunk American looking for the Beer of Oranges, or some such nonsense.

Fire, smoke, and ash were the only companions on the way to the old vineyard. It took several days to make the journey, hampered by the need for obscurity. The two reached the old vineyard property at night, in fact, Lord M wasn't sure if he had reached the property at all. If he had, the vines had been burned down long ago. Was the guesthouse still there? Clouds parted enough for moonlight to shine through and there, yes, the guesthouse was still there. But strangely enough, it was surrounded by carriage remnants, as if the carriages had been taken from nobility and broken in violence.

"We must go to the guesthouse," Lord M said. "There is an old caretaker there. He can explain this."

The two reached the guesthouse but were immediately dissuaded from entering by a strong odor of death. So overwhelming was the toxic air that Lord M had to stop and turn the other way.

"I will go," Joie said to Lord M's amazement. "I have walked this path before."

Joie attempted to open a door, but it was jammed. She then began walking around back, but she stopped.

"I hear someone coming," she said.

Joie spoke soft French and walked toward a figure approaching toward the side of the house. Lord M, however, pulled his shirt up over his mouth and made a determined effort for the guesthouse while Joie met up with the figure. It turned out that Joie and the figure were able to hold an amicable conversation, though in low tones to avoid possible detection from unknown mobs that might be lurking.

Lord M threw himself against the front door to unjam it. But Joie was given urgent advice by the unknown figure, and she in turn rushed toward Lord M, telling him to stop, though she had to hush her urgent plea, again to prevent imagined lurking mobs from possibly attacking.

"Do not go in. Do not!" she finally yelled, throwing caution to the wind.

It was too late. Lord M entered. He instinctively reached for a hidden panel meant for just such occasions, where he found (still there) a candle and small tinder box. He lit the candle and looked.

"Do not look!" Joie called as she approached the door from outside.

Lord M attempted to understand what his eyes were showing him. Clothing of people covering shapes. Was this a prank? Had someone fashioned dummies and clothed them? These dummies had no heads. Yet they stank like the ends of the Earth. And now a new sense took hold. These clothes were familiar. Very familiar.

"Leave now!" Joie said as she grabbed hold of Lord M's arm and led him away with the candle still in hand.

The two exited the house, and Joie led Lord M back toward the figure. Lord M held the candle up. Who was this figure? After careful study, he realized it was the old caretaker, but who was now emaciated, being but a wispy skeletal frame. He had a walking stick for help, a stick that had perhaps the same diameter as his own leg.

"It is not safe here," the caretaker said. "Please follow me."

The caretaker began to walk away from the guesthouse, albeit slowly. Joie was about to follow, but she realized Lord M remained transfixed as he stared back at the guesthouse, in shock. Joie took the candle from him and urged him along. Still he would not budge.

"Carry him," she said to Lord M. "Make good this deed on your soul and carry him."

Lord M carried the caretaker, who directed the two to a little hut where the caretaker and his family lived. All were thin beyond health, but they were at least alive. Joie produced food from her pack and shared it with all. The caretaker's wife was able to take this food and make it quite presentable on an eating table with clean water. Light and heat from a fireplace further welcomed them.

The caretaker and his family ate hungrily. Joie ate more leisurely, while Lord M's appetite was completely withdrawn. The caretaker's wife managed to get some tea going, and Lord M had a bit of that at Joie's insistence.

"We have no spirits, I'm afraid to say," the caretaker said. "Thank you for the food."

The caretaker sent his wife and children into another room where they continued to nourish themselves on Joie's provisions.

"Hardy?" Joie said.

The caretaker looked at Joie in surprise.

"This is Lord Mortison Hardshore, a citizen of Britain," the caretaker said.

"Are you not Hardy, the American?" Joie asked.

"No," Lord M said. "I...I..."

"I know why you have come," the caretaker said. "Lord M. I wanted to send word. I tried. We could not."

The caretaker then explained to Joie about how Lord M used to own the vineyard, of the neighboring DeBlanche family, and how the vineyard was sold to the DeBlanches with the stipulation he be kept on as the main caretaker. He also explained how Baron DeBlanche reneged on his word, treated him poorly, and had others mismanage the vineyard against his wishes.

"I am sorry to hear of your misfortune," Joie said. "But there is more, isn't there."

The caretaker nodded his head in affirmation. Lord M looked directly at the caretaker with a stare of hardy defiance.

"I cannot deny what your eyes have seen," the caretaker said.

"The entire DeBlanche family? Including..." Lord M tried to finish.

The caretaker nodded again in the affirmative. He wanted to speak further, but he suddenly choked on food.

"I'm not used to eating with fine company," the caretaker said. "Brother has turned against brother. It sickens me beyond hope."

"They were beheaded," Lord M finally acknowledged.

The caretaker tried to hush Lord M's words on such matter, but Lord M would not be silenced.

"I had to say that. I had to see for myself," Lord M said. "I wanted to bring Lady Antoinette back to England for...for...I loved her. I was a fool to let her slip from me. But she has. At the hands of...animals. Why do such vile filth destroy the beauty this country once had? Why give a country a name, only to have it desecrated? I was too petty to think of France as my little playground for my own selfish desires. I...am lost here. Even a sense of vengeance fails me."

"We must leave," Joie said.

Lord M paused, sighed, and said, "We will return to Damien."

The caretaker shuddered.

"Damien DeVille?" he asked.

"Yes," Lord M said. "Have you heard of him?"

The caretaker cleared his throat and attempted to speak, but instead he fell into a coughing fit.

"He gave me safe passage to France from England," Lord M said.

"He may have given you passage, but there is nothing safe about him," the caretaker said. "He has sold out innocent French people to whoever will believe his lies. Do not return to him. He will not return you to England. At least not alive."

"What will he do?" Lord M asked.

Joie wanted to speak but dared not.

"Is that not enough of an answer?" the caretaker said. "You might end up dead. Or working in a remote corner of the Earth as a slave. He only fulfills half of any bargain."

"What about you, Joie?" Lord M asked.

"I could read his eyes when we left him," she said. "My use to him has come to an end."

"He will kill you?" Lord M asked in surprise.

"Not directly," Joie said. "One of his men would do the job. But he would watch and rate the killing technique. In fact, he often has several old slaves be killed at once by several different men. The man with the best technique gets his own reward."

"I should return and have him killed," Lord M said.

"You cannot," the caretaker said. "His connections run too far. Best you return to England by another way."

"But how?" Lord M asked.

The caretaker whispered something into Joie's ear. She nodded.

"I will guide you to friends in this matter," Joie said.

The caretaker agreed to stay behind to allay any suspicion should Damien's men come round. Joie then led Lord M to a route that the caretaker had whispered into her ear. A kind of French underground assisted them in this trip, which took them not to the Bay of Biscay, but instead to Spain, where Spanish friendlies made arrangements for Lord M's return to England. Joie herself, however, remained with Spanish friends, where she could help other despondent French escape from the turmoil in France.

The ship ride to England, though safe for Lord M, took a mental toll upon his psyche. His mind pieced together what he had seen in the guesthouse. So powerful was this image in his mind, so powerful indeed, that the image remained in his waking vision while staring directly at the ocean. The image, without doubt, was of the headless bodies of Baron DeBlanche, his financier, and of Lady Antoinette. Words from the caretaker filled his mind, words that he had not paid attention to at the time but that now bubbled up in his thoughts, that the DeBlanche family hid in the guesthouse in hopes of avoiding the march of death upon the nobility.

Lord M was both crushed and mystified, angry yet cloistered. The vision of incomplete bodies left him incomplete and swimming as if lost in the vast ocean before him, waiting to become whole again for a passing sea creature to consume him in one gulp for the dignity of death. Instead, he felt the emptiness of a zombie-like creature, paralyzed into forced existence. His mind was so distanced from reality that he could not remember reaching England nor how he returned to his estate. His last point of sanity, as one might have while peering toward a distant star of wished-for divinity, was that of his magical moment of pure essence with Lady A in the grotto.

Chapter 11:
A Sense of Business

Lord M remained secluded in the country with his mother helping with Lily. By age five, Lily's oversight was relegated to the servants. She spent time watching them work, whether it be cooking, cleaning, sewing, mending, gardening, or general maintenance. She didn't help so much as she watched.

And so, the years passed. Lily received a standard education as dictated to nobility of the time (for which Lord M's mother felt was a waste of money), but Lily realized she knew quite a bit more from watching the workers. She noticed the servants knew a number of tricks of the trade to make things easier, but the only way to learn was to spend time with them, as they never wrote down this knowledge. Lily also noticed how much effort was spent in manual labor, and given the emergence of the steam engine, it seemed a natural fit for helping the servants do the manual labor instead of spending lots of time trying to recover from being overworked.

There was something else Lily noticed. The nobility purposely separated themselves from the working people, with the nobility believing one should aspire to purity of the stars in the sky and remain uncontaminated by the practical but "distasteful" world of the "ordinary". Lily thought this star worship ironic since these stars could not be seen during the labors of the daytime. Lily would look up to the blue sky and see sun, cloud, rain, and snow. She watched how rain gave water for plants and animals, sunshine gave growth.

Lily would watch the cooks bring a kettle to a boil, and envisioned the steam being her own little cloud maker, but she realized the steam only escaped. She would have the silversmith make little spinners to fit on the end of the kettle spout to move and make sound when the water was hot enough. Lily marveled at how the steam could produce such an effect, while the cook was happy he could do other things while waiting for the water to boil.

We return then to Lily as she was at 16 years of age, after just having heard Carmichael tell a shorter version of the stories told here, about Lord M's visit to France to sell the vineyard up to this moment in late summer of 1805.

"Mr. Carmichael," Lily said, "I have always wondered about the household finances."

Carmichael looked at Lily in surprise. A girl of 16 asking about finances? About things mathematical? It seemed a fancy of the moment, but, to take his mind off the recent failed venture, decided to humor Lily. He explained about cash flow and how money is invested to generate good cash flow. The trick is to make good investments and to avoid bad investments.

"What is the best way to do that?" Lily asked.

"Some people have good intuition, others do not," Carmichael answered.

"Is intuition the best way?" Lily asked. "You are always working with numbers in your little books. What about those? What is the best way to work with those numbers? To get the best investment?"

Carmichael was surprised. What was the best way? Even he wasn't sure. His ventures with Lord M had turned out so poorly that he doubted his own skills. And so, he steered her to the local mathematician, Mr. Adams, for that answer.

Lily sent word for a meeting with Mr. Adams, who lived in the nearby town in a small house between a school and a church. Mr. Adams, a retired schoolteacher, happily accepted.

On the day of the meeting, Lily gathered up as many newspapers as she could and called for a carriage to take her into town.

"I'm sorry. There is a delay," was the reply.

The main carriage had already been spoken for by Lord M for his own business, the secondary carriage for Lord M's mother, and other carriages were in various states of repair. Lily checked with the stable master for a horse, as Lily had the idea of riding a horse into town, but the stable master was quick to point out that this was undignified.

"I must find a way into town," Lily said aloud, though she thought no one heard.

"I know a way," said a woman with dark hair and mid complexion. "I'm Hannah Balfrey, the horse hand helper. I exercise these horses daily. You're Lily."

"Yes," Lily said. "I have a meeting in town with Mr. Adams. I was hoping to borrow a horse."

But Lily was so saddled with her satchel of newspapers and such that she struggled to move around. Hannah smiled, took the satchel from Lily, and motioned for Lily to follow her. The two walked into what appeared to be another horse stall in the stable but in fact led to a secret door to a secret room where a two-wheeled horse cart somewhat resembling a chariot was stored.

"This is a curricle, a fast horse cart that some male visitors borrow for quick runs around the countryside," Hannah said.

"I'll take it. I need a horse, though. Is it safe?" Lily asked.

"No. Quite dangerous at speed," Hannah said. "It takes *two* horses, and not just any horses. They must work carefully together. But I know which two. You may help if you like. Oh, and I will drive. Watch me with my disguise."

Hannah adorned herself with a disguise quickly retrieved from a hidden compartment.

"Now I'm one of those *male* drivers," she said.

Lily laughed. The two worked quickly enough to team up the two horses to the curricle. It was then off into town, at a pace much quicker than Lily had anticipated.

"Don't worry," Hannah said. "I've had plenty of experience with this curricle and these horses. We won't go too quickly, but we shan't dawdle either."

Speedy but not rushed, Hannah took Lily to the town in the curricle. The horses worked well under Hannah's control and provided a pleasant ride. A town caretaker tended to the horses as Hannah chaperoned Lily to Mr. Adams's front door. Three knocks to the door later, an older gentleman arrived. It was Mr. Adams himself!

"Hello! I'm Mr. Adams!" he said.

"I'm Lily," Lily said, "and this is—"

"Hank," Hannah said, still in disguise.

"Hello, Lily and Hank! Won't you come in?" Mr. Adams said.

"Thank you," Hannah and Lily replied.

The three sat down briefly for tea and cakes, with Lily going on about her newspapers.

"My satchel!" she said, suddenly realizing it was still in the curricle.

"I'll fetch it," Hannah said with a deep voice.

With the satchel fetched, Lily pulled out her newspapers and spread them out before Mr. Adams. Lily asked many questions at once about investing, leaving Mr. Adams a bit surprised and overwhelmed by the 16 year old.

"The first thing is not to be so overwhelmed, and group things by a system," he said.

Mr. Adams showed how to look for newspapers with information about trading while skipping over newspapers that had only agenda to purport.

"Numbers do not have agenda, but they do have meaning," Mr. Adams said.

It was only a few more seconds before Lily honed in on financial papers, particularly *Lloyd's List*, which contained not only information on financials like stocks and exchanges, but also a marine list of maritime trade. This particular list fascinated Lily.

Hannah, being a handy horse helper and happy harness driver, was quite taken aback by Lily's ability to quickly discuss such mathematics with Mr. Adams. Mr. Adams, not wishing to leave "Hank" unattended, offered Hannah a smoke and a chance for billiards with fellow visitors in another room, to which Hannah agreed.

While Lily excelled at math with Mr. Adams, Hannah performed poorly at billiards. Part of the problem was that Hannah had never played before and had to learn the rules. Tired of losing repeatedly, Hannah was ready to leave. She thanked the fellows and sought for Lily. Mr. Adams, as it turned out, was tired too, though Lily still had questions for him.

"My dear Lily," Mr. Adams said, "you surprise me with so many questions. But the most important lesson to learn is how to plan. You are welcome to come back, but it must be part of a plan. I'll draw up what I think you should learn, and you do the same. Come back again, and we'll compare plans."

Lily agreed. The two returned to Lord M's country estate, worried that their absence would become an issue. As it turned out, it was not. In fact, when Lord M found out, he was pleased that Lily had found a new hobby that kept her out of his affairs and freed him to pursue his gardening when not occupied with the next failed venture.

The next day, Lily gathered up other literature from Lord M's estate she felt worthy of financial study. She approached Hannah again for a ride into town.

"I would like to take the buggy into town," Lily said, "or what did you call it? A cuticle?"

"A curricle," Hannah smiled. "But I should drive again. It's not safe for you to take the team in by yourself. Lord M—"

"I love my father, but he doesn't pay me mind," Lily said.

"I will take you in. Perhaps we can work on your horsemanship skills," Hannah said.

"Will you let me drive? Part of the way?" Lily asked.

Hannah smiled again. She teamed the horses to the curricle and took Lily into town, allowing Lily occasional control of the horses while providing instruction. Lily made an excellent pupil, to which Hannah was pleasantly surprised.

"I might have you help out with training the horses," Hannah half joked.

"Would you really? Let me race them!" Lily said with excitement.

"Oh, that was meant for levity!" Hannah said. "Women aren't allowed to race horses."

Lily grinned.

"Lily!" Hannah cautioned.

"You're right," Lily said. "My business studies come first. Still, if ever I need a break, there must be a quick steed ready for speed."

The two exchanged giggles.

Lily and Hannah continued with these visits into town on a near-daily basis. Lily very quickly learned advanced mathematics such as algebra, geometry, trigonometry, and statistics. Lily compiled data from her newspapers and other printed matter and then created graphs and charts of all sorts.

After such sessions on the way home, Lily could visualize all the things she had studied during the day and could recall past lessons in her mind and create visual data maps. Hannah was quite impressed with this effort but was also quite sad.

"Why are you sad?" Lily asked.

"I keep losing in billiards," Hannah lamented.

Lily had an idea, and she acted on it. She had a special secret room constructed in the stable to house a billiard table. There, Lily watched Hannah's play, took notes, and applied her math lessons from Mr. Adams to chart performance and discover where Hannah could improve.

Hannah did improve. Visitors of Mr. Adams soon noticed that not only did "Hank" become more competitive, but "he" actually won a few games. It came time then for these gentlemen competitors to place wagers to make the games more interesting. Hannah did not have much money and was only willing to wager a little, and she was quickly coerced into betting double-or-nothing until she lost all her winnings.

Lily focused her lessons more on statistics and probability with Mr. Adams. On rides home to the estate, Lily would explain her idea that bets should be better "planned" as a part of strategy of gaining knowledge from each bet and using that to place better future bets. The double-or-nothing bet was immediately ruled out, and instead a progressive style of larger or smaller bets were to be placed based on all sorts of statistics and calculated probabilities that Lily had worked out during their stable billiard meetings.

Hannah very quickly made money and held onto it during these billiard games. It wasn't long before visitors from neighboring towns heard of "Hank" and soon referred to "him" as "Slyman the Shark" or just "Hank Slyman".

Hank Slyman received more competition, and Lily was happy to chart these games and provide advice on both wager and play. In this way, Lily developed her first sense of business.

Chapter 12:

Excellent Cloth

Helping Hannah with billiard bets was one thing, but working up an honest business was another, and Lily was determined to invest in one.

Lily's grandmother (Lord M's mother) continued to take a dim view of Lily, often seeing Lily as making a fool of herself.

"Deranged girl," the grandmother would often say. "She is unable to grasp the ways of the world. A charity case."

In a desire to "motivate Lily out of the nest," the grandmother gave Lily a small sum (a benefaction originally intended for charity) to be used as enticement to a future husband, "so that he may deal with her cerebral imbalance." A benefaction was the only money the grandmother was willing to offer since, "No two-blood shall receive an inheritance."

Lily instead was eager to invest this amount based on her studies with Mr. Adams.

Hannah had moved on from simple billiard games in Mr. Adams's house to more public games in the town pub. Hannah as "Slyman Shark" changed her strategy to purposely win or lose from time to time to attract players, who she plied with beer or pressured with lost bets to get information. In this way, she learned that a local sheep farmer was not doing well and was preparing to sell his farm for a pittance.

Lily was sure she could make money off the situation. She visited the farm and sweet-talked her way with the farmer and his sheep while quietly studying how he fed his flock, how he tended them, how he sheared them, and who he sold the wool to.

On return to the Hardshore estate, Hannah and Lily met in the stable billiard room. Lily charted out her business plan, deciding that she would invest in the farmer's wool business, but she would make changes as part of the agreement. She would need to find better and cheaper food, as the sheep had overgrazed and were emaciated. Second, she would need to find a better place for cleaning and spinning the wool.

Hannah went into town to make more inquiries over billiards and beer while Lily went to Carmichael with her business plan. Mr. Carmichael was quite surprised to hear Lily bring up such a proposition, as she was just a "girl", but on further review, he admitted the plan had potential—provided she could solve the problem of cheap food and better processing and spinning. But he cautioned Lily that her biggest problem was yet to come.

"I doubt anyone would make a business deal with you, no matter how much money you have," he said.

Lily was shocked and surprised to hear this. She walked outside to ask her father about this nitpicky point, but Lord M told her to put the thought out of her mind since she was just a girl. Next, Lily went to her grandmother to ask the same thing, and her grandmother admitted that yes, if Lily had been a boy, business deals could be made. That was why her grandmother had a boy, Lord M, to make business deals.

"Business deals he made," Grandmother said, "but as for being good, that he did not make."

Lily returned to see Carmichael, but before she did, Hannah showed up. The two walked in together to see Carmichael. There, Hannah admitted she'd found a farmer who had excess food that would go to waste because he didn't have the animals to harvest the crop, and he couldn't afford to hire help. As for better cleaning and spinning, Hannah admitted that the job of cleaning was smelly and unpleasant, and the few who would clean the wool wanted top money. But Hannah learned of some nuns who might be willing to clean and spin the wool in return for compensation sent to their school.

"I asked on your behalf, not mentioning you by name," Hannah said, "but the crop farmer and sheep farmer both said they wouldn't do business with you, because you're not a MAN."

"Lily Marie Hardshore. I am sorry," Carmichael said.

"I never knew your middle name," Hannah said.

"L M Hardshore. Like my father," Lily said with a sudden idea and a great smile like a cat that had swallowed a canary.

"Oh no," Carmichael said, suddenly picking up on Lily's idea.

"Can it be any worse than the other Hardshore ventures?" Lily pointed out. "Besides, it's my own money. Nothing will be lost from the estate."

"You know how other estates go," Carmichael said.

"Yes. Girls with a benefaction hold onto it until they surrender it to a new husband," Lily said. "That's not for me. I want you to draw up the papers, Mr. Carmichael, for L M Hardshore Associates. All deals are to be done by letter. We'll start with these farmers and the nuns. They will think they are doing business with my father. Only you and Hannah will know it is me. I must ask you both for oaths of secrecy."

Both gave their oaths.

"Good," Lily grinned. "First order of business is to hire Hank Slyman as a courier."

Lily and Hannah laughed to Carmichael's bemusement.

"Who is this person?" Carmichael said.

"Write up the letter, and I'll deliver it," Lily said.

Carmichael wrote up the letter.

"Pass this on to Mr. Slyman," Lily said, passing the note to Hannah.

Lily and Hannah laughed again.

Carmichael simply shrugged his shoulders without further ado.

It was this way then. L M Hardshore Associates purchased the sheep farm and hired the farmer as farm manager. Arrangements were made with the crop farmer to provide feed to the sheep farmer. The nuns were advised of wool that would arrive soon, and so they prepared to clean and spin it. Carmichael drew up all documents. Hannah delivered them. Lily planned, charted progress, examined results along the way, charted further, planned again, and so on.

The first shearing came, and the wool was sent to the nuns. Cleaning and processing took longer than expected, as the sheep did not start off in the best of shape. The processed wool was sold, and the business broke even. The sheep farmer was so happy that (being allowed to keep the sheep dairy products as part of the deal), he sent an especially well-produced block of cheese to the L M Hardshore Associates in gratitude.

The second shearing came, and the wool was much better. By this time, Lily had charted which parts of the processing gave the nuns the most difficulty. It was the cleaning and spinning. "Hank Slyman" was sent to play billiards and find machine owners who, down on their luck from billiards or other bad business, would allow Hank Slyman to "acquire" such equipment at low (or no) cost.

Some of this equipment contained primitive steam engines. Lily studied these, refined their design, and had L M Hardshore Associates hire a millwright to rework them to her specifications.

The result was that the spun thread from the second go-round was of much better quality than the first, so much so that people were asking what kind of special animals provided such thread. Cashmere? Merino? No official explanation was given from L M Hardshore Associates, only that it was from "the finest wool available". The secret, however, was in how the wool was cleaned and prepared. Lily had learned of the manual methods of people stepping on smelly concoctions for unhealthy lengths of time. She had machines not only do this work, but do so in clever processes that gave the wool a more refined texture.

All made money. Lily added a special percentage to Hannah's pay, making Hannah more than just a hired hand. As it turned out, since Mr. Carmichael was the same person handling the affairs for L M Hardshore

Associates and Lord M's ventures, Lord M's money increased as well.

It should be said that when matters of hiring came about, Lily of course was prime to "interview" said candidates. Spending years listening to men of shady repute swindle money from her father, she developed a keen ear for the honest and not so much. Lily did not hire every candidate that she encountered. Nay, oft came the ones recommended from Hannah's billiard play only to be rejected by Lily for their subtle dishonest ways that could not be so cleverly hidden.

Of course acceptance and rejection came from letters by the "association". Lily never presented herself as the one actively involved, only as the one delivering the news by document as occasion met, or delivered by "Hank" on others.

Lily's accomplishments were not achieved in mere days, weeks, or months. In fact, they took several years. And as these years passed, other changes came along. The nuns had greater need for paper for schools, and so Lily had separate management and facilities drawn up to process the wool. Further, Lily ventured into the weaving and paper-producing industries, both as a follow-up to thread production and to supply paper for the nuns' schools.

In fact, other schools were asking for Hardshore paper, as Lily could produce such at a lower price than others. And so, Lily invested part of her gains in creating schools for girls, so that these girls would have an education and a better future. Many of these girls would go to work for L M Hardshore Associates, and so it was a good investment for Lily.

Lily also created an association for the house staff as several wanted to send their children to school for better futures. Lily helped them establish accounts for their retirements.

Life with L M Hardshore Associates sailed with such smoothness that Lily was surprised to hear that her co-owners of a tin mine in Cornwall were asking for more control of the mining company to improve productivity. Lily had 51% ownership in the company so that she could have the final say in decisions, but day-to-day details were managed by the co-owners.

"Tin mines in Cornwall are common," Carmichael said. "You could sell your stake and move on to another."

"This one puzzles me, Carmichael," Lily said. "I think I should visit the mine first to see if I should sell my stake. The co-owners might be hiding something from me. They might be cheating me."

Lily called for Hannah, and it was set. The two would travel to Cornwall.

Chapter 13:

Roy and the Gunpowder Pirates

Hannah as "Hank" accompanied Lily to Cornwall, a region at the southwest corner of England. They settled their things at Stone Circle Inn. After doing so, they first toured the inn itself. Lily marveled at its stone construction, while Hannah used her conversational skills with strangers to get information.

"Stone for the inn and other buildings is readily available from local mining," Hannah explained to Lily as the two walked around. "The inn has a circle of stone around it, see? This is to celebrate the many stone circles in the area."

"We are close to the sea. I should like to take a look," Lily said.

The two took a walk onto a dock and looked to the west onto what would someday be called the Celtic Sea. But for them, it was just the Atlantic Ocean.

"Did I tell you, Hannah, about the dream I had last night? And the night before? About ships. Ships on the ocean. I feel there is something to that, that ships play some part in my future."

"They may," Hannah said.

The two had just stepped off the dock when a group of boys of various ages showed up carrying a dummy made of stuffed straw into old clothing.

"Penny for Guy!" they called out.

Intrigued, Lily walked up to them and promised them a penny for an explanation. They told of their need for fireworks for the upcoming celebration of Gunpowder Treason Day, which was to be held tomorrow, November the 5th.

"The Thanksgiving Act. Guy Fawkes Night," Hannah said to Lily, who suddenly remembered the significance of the attempt on King James 1 and his parliament in 1605.

Lily donated several additional pennies.

"May 1 know your name to whom 1 donate?" Lily asked the eldest boy, who looked nearly 18 years of age.

"My name is Roy," he said. "Captain Roy Finchley. We are the Gunpowder Pirates."

The boys laughed and cheered.

"Where is your ship?" Lily asked.

"We don't have one yet," Roy said. "But we will. As soon as we save up enough pennies. We will buy one! And sail the seven seas, raiding other ships of gunpowder for our fireworks!"

"Hooray!" the boys cheered. "Hooray for fireworks!"

"One should not steal for fireworks," Lily said. "One should learn an honest trade and earn money properly."

Hannah was surprised to see Lily giving such a lecture to these boys. But the boys, though dirty and grimy, showed a youthful exuberance that charmed her. Roy explained that his fellow "pirates" were already skilled artisans, being able to make such excellent fireworks and explosives, that their learning was already complete. It was their time to seize and slay the world, at least those parts that wanted to use gunpowder for evil. The boys only wanted to use gunpowder to bring excitement and joy to peoples' lives. They were so adamant about this fact that they insisted Lily and "Hank" stay in the area and attend the November 5th celebration.

"How did you know I was from out of town?" Lily asked.

"By the accent," Roy replied.

Another chuckle amongst the new friends. Lily had quite forgotten her original intent for visiting Cornwall, to see about her 51% stake in the mine, and Hannah, seeing Lily taking a much needed rest from her business machinations, allowed the forgetfulness to continue and for Lily to slip into the celebratory mood.

Hannah and Lily then relaxed as much as they could, but every so often, the effect of mining crept toward their purview. Hannah often recognized it first—the echoes of mining work, the occasional mining worker walking their way, or a mining implement cast aside—and she did what she could to distract Lily of such elements.

Tomorrow came around. Hannah and Lily paid a brief visit to a church that had just let out after having read the Thanksgiving Act. The church air was somber yet hopeful, musty yet airy. Lily walked up to a small devotional table, with a portrait of King James I along with the Holy Bible in his name. A piece of paper had been folded up and placed in the Bible. Lily opened the Bible to see that the paper was set in 1st Kings near a phrase, "God Save the King." Further, the paper itself had a copy of the Thanksgiving Act with a particular phrase highlighted: "Gunpowder : An Invention so inhuman, barbarous and cruel, as the like was never before heard of."

"We studied about the Gunpowder Plot against King James I, but I never paid it much mind until now," Lily said.

"The day is not well celebrated by your father or his estate. He still dreams of reaching the sky to a distant past of his own," Hannah said. "I am surprised to see you reflecting on the times of King James I. It is a side I am not used to seeing."

Lily returned the paper to the Bible and both to the table.

"I don't like how it makes me feel," Lily said. "People become too lost in these things when instead they should be attending to issues of the day. Let's return to open sunlight."

They left the church, but given the time of year, the daylight was already fading. Evening festivities had been in the works, and so Hannah directed Lily to them, where small meals had been set up in tents around a large circle of stones. The meals were a special foodstuff of sorts rolled up in a crust, often with no hint as to their contents. Some were meat pies while others were proper sweets. Quite often the joke went around of a person being presented one kind only to find out it was another.

As dusk approached, small bonfires were lit inside the circle of stones. The stones heated up from both inside the circle and out, as the tents acted as a thermal barrier and reflected the heat back toward the circle. The circle became quite the celebratory place of warmth, while those who ventured outside and past the tents rediscovered the coolness of Cornwall. But Cornwall was never so cold as to cause frostbite, and so whatever temporary misery endured was quickly allayed by returning to the circle.

Lily noticed several of the young women and even the girls going up to the stones and hugging them.

"It's for good luck," Hannah said. "Try it."

Lily did so. Immediately, she felt the strength of the stone hold steady her stance while warmth from the stone permeated her body. She fell into a light daze and half-fancied walking side-by-side with the moving statue of a horse. She heard a "Pop!" and her senses returned, as an eager child had jumped ahead of the festivities by tossing a small firework into one of the fires.

"Not yet!" called someone else. "It is time for the entertainment. Pirates?"

Then from one of the tents on the far side of the circle came forth Roy and his Gunpowder Pirates. Hannah by now had procured two stools, one for Lily and one for herself. Lily sat on the stool and leaned against the warm stone pillar, watching as the performance unfolded. Roy's group was dressed in pirate attire and carried along decorative flat props, giving the illusion they were sailing along in their pirate ship. They "sailed" around the various bonfires that had been set, chanting and singing about how proud they were to be pirates, taking from the bad and giving to the good.

Another group of children came along in another such "boat" of their own, carrying along the flat prop and pretending to exchange in gun battle with Roy's

Pirate Boat. The two groups set off a firework each to mimic the guns of a boat, and Roy's group won. The losing "boat" deposited their boat props in the center of the circle. One by one, other such "boats" came out to seek battle against Roy's group, and each time Roy's group won. The pile became higher and higher, and still another group came out and fashioned a quick platform of sorts out of the retired props. This group worked as if working in a mine, pretending to dig for ore with mock strokes of the pick and pretending to find great fortune while pulling up piece after piece in building the platform.

A strange feeling came over Lily, as if she were watching more than just a fanciful play. Were these children playfully mocking what they saw around them? Or were they reenacting something they lived day to day? Certainly they weren't pirates from day to day, but the mining part. Hmm. It planted a seed in her mind, and she suddenly remembered her original reason for visiting Cornwall—her stake in the mine. But whatever guilt she might have felt over the delay in pursuing her original purpose was replaced with a sense of honest discovery that could not be acquired in a more direct request of the co-owners. And it hit upon her—she might be dealing with child labor. With her own mine.

In anger, she ripped a leg from her stool. The stool wobbled in toward the stone. She took the leg and whacked it against the stone, as far up as she could reach while still sitting. The stone absorbed the shockwave as if it were being asked a question, the shockwave split and traveled both up and down, bounced off its top and bottom, returned, and sent its reply to Lily, who was still leaning against it. And the reply was anger too, as if in agreement with her.

She repeated the swat. Others, thinking her swatting was a part of the performance (and a good idea) began swatting legs of stools against other objects as well—the stones, other stools, tables—anything that could add to the growing group chant and wail as if all were back in 1605 and preparing to battle the Traitors of England.

The group building the platform had finished. They hurriedly waved for people to throw things at them. What? It was only a few moments before effigy upon effigy of Guy Fawkes was tossed, hoisted, or carried to the top of the platform.

A horn sounded. The performers scattered from the platform. The wail of the audience increased. A horn sounded again, and what looked like a cannon was rolled into the circle. Roy's pirates pointed the cannon barrel up to the sky. Roy drew his sword and held it to the sky as well. Several horns now blew, and the audience was ecstatic with excitement. In one stroke, Roy drew his sword downward and caught the fuse of the cannon, igniting it.

The cannon sent flash and bang high into the air, a veritable fountain of flame with a puffball pinnacle, hovering, waiting, as if only supported by the fountain of flame shooting upward from the cannon, like a water fountain supporting a toy boat while balance and steadiness prevailed. The puffball itself then fashioned itself into a flaming pirate boat, and as it did, it became too heavy to be sustained by the fountain of flame.

The fountain of flame went out, and the flaming pirate boat dropped dead out of the sky. Audience reaction became a mixture of dropping wails in celebration to yells of delight to screams of fear that they would be consumed by this flame of a ship.

As the flaming boat descended, it seemed to grow larger. The crowd panicked. All left the inner part of the stone circle. Some hid in their tents, some dropped to the ground, and some hid behind the stone structures. The stones themselves seemed to move in toward the center, impossible yes, but that was how Lily perceived the event, because she had stood by now and had tried to lean against her stone structure for strength, but she kept falling behind it.

The flaming pirate ship landed, and landed it did—right next to the platform (and narrowly missing the effigies of Guy Fawkes). The effigies seemed to laugh, as if they were the target (they were) but that they had escaped proper judgement the way the real Guy Fawkes had "fallen" off a platform to avoid proper hanging and such. One could attribute the laughing sound to the creaking of the platform as the falling flame of pirate ship had glanced off it, but the sound was too real for the people to ignore, and they went from panic to rage. Many threw sticks and stones at the effigies. Some even tried to rush the platform and climb it to maim the effigies, deservedly so.

But those who had rushed the platform were in for a surprise. The flaming pirate ship set the platform afire, and it raged quickly, sending those rushers back to the outside of the circle. Not for long. The sudden rise of air vents caused the effigies to shudder and dance. It was worse than the laughter, because it seemed these effigies were more active and in fact could at any moment jump off the platform and wreak havoc amongst the people.

The people became quite concerned. Roy himself seemed to sweat the occasion, and many were calling for him to be boxed at the ears.

"King James!" Roy shouted.

Roy's group during this mayhem had reloaded the cannon. They fired the cannon high into the air, and after several seconds, a shape took form like that of a golden eagle. It was the national bird of Scotland, and rightly so, as from Scotland took on the shape of King James, who now descended from the heavens like a Messenger of God. He had the Holy Bible in one hand and his sword in the other.

"Heathens!" he shouted.

King James, flying with speed toward the effigies of Guy Fawkes, threw his Holy Bible at them. The effigies screamed in fright just before they were squashed downward into the fiery platform of flame. The platform seemed to explode with fire. Indeed, it became a great fireball pushing upward, engulfing platform and effigies in its wake, though Lily thought she caught the glimpse of an effigy or two being exploded upward and away from the now-collapsing platform.

King James then sent his sword through the fireball and into the nearly defunct platform, and that shattered things for good, sending hissing embers upward into a beautiful kaleidoscope of colors coalescing into multiple rainbows. Pleased, King James reverted to eagle form and flew away.

"All Englishmen are free!" Roy shouted.

The people echoed his sentiment, but with the main show now ended, the people fell into disorganized activity of eating (much needed after the excite and fright), drinking (also much needed), and dancing. A small band of musicians came out to play, and the mood settled into welcome harmony. Roy himself, who was initially chided during his presentation, received many congratulations for his performance. Indeed, Lily and Hannah made it a point to offer their own congratulations to Roy.

"That is the best value for my penny ever invested," Lily said to Roy. "Why, with such investments, you could become a valuable member of my...of my father's organization. Such a clever young man. All with gunpowder?"

Roy grinned.

"I cannot take all credit, of course," he said. "My Gunpowder Pirates are experts in crafting fireworks of all kinds. Properly controlled and respected, gunpowder can be harnessed to perform all sorts of works to the good."

"You have a strong head on your shoulders," Hannah as Hank said. "But what do you make of the church service today, the mention that gunpowder is, 'An Invention so inhuman, barbarous and cruel, as the like was never before heard of.' ?"

"I don't attend church," Roy said with a smirk.

His pirate group laughed.

"Those were words echoed by King James," Hannah added. "Further, he was against the Magna Carta, believing kings to be little gods on Earth. It came to a head with the English Civil War when his son, Charles I—"

"I think we can take the spirit of King James for its proper intent," Lily said to salvage the conversation. "I would like to hear more about your fireworks craftsmanship. Do you have a factory? Will you show me what you know?"

Roy was more than delighted to stroll around with Lily and explain his various devices, starting with the cannon and including other such behind-the-scenes works. Hannah as Hank tagged along at first, but her words against King James, though not ill-meant, tended to leave her out of conversations. Lily at length said that Hannah (Hank) could stroll around and turn in early if needed, that she would be fine with Roy and his group, that she trusted these humble Cornwall people.

Hannah was at first opposed, but she agreed. In fact, she was a bit tired. She headed back for the inn. Darkness was about her, so there was little light by which she could see. In fact, as she left the bonfires behind, she only had the lights of the inn to guide her, and she found herself stumbling along unknown ground. She tripped over something and fell. Pulling herself up, she wanted to know what she tripped over, which she picked up and held in her hand. She could not quite see what it was, as it was still too dark, but it was somewhat soft, like a light pillow, and it had strands of glowing straw embers here and there. None burned her, as they were too weak, but they continued to burn nonetheless, like a deposed puppet leader having his last draught of tobacco.

She held onto this "puppet leader" until she reached the inn, at which point she realized she had acquired the head of a Guy Fawkes effigy.

"That was quite an explosion to send it that far," Hannah said. "I'll keep it as a souvenir to show Lily in the morning."

But then Hannah studied the effigy remnant more closely. Affixed to the head either by craft or by explosion, Hannah didn't know which, was a bit of cloth, perhaps a collar or upper garment remnant, with the embroidered letters, "L M Hardshore Associates".

"Fancy that clothing from one of Lily's textile mills made its way down here," Hannah mused.

But the same numb-chilly wind that caught Lily earlier had now taken hold of Hannah.

"Could this be...could the children have taken this clothing from the mines? From Lily's mine?" Hannah mused.

It wasn't until the next day that Hannah showed the effigy remnant to Lily, who herself had returned to the inn too late for Hannah to receive properly, as Hannah had fallen asleep. But this was morning. After showing the effigy to Lily, and having a brief conversation about Hannah's trip back, Lily agreed the two should continue to discuss the matter over breakfast.

Over breakfast, Lily recounted what she learned from Roy, that he and his "pirates" worked in a tin mine, though out of fear he did not say which one, as the foreman would whip their hides raw. Roy himself would be 18 years of age soon, and he was weighing his next career. He so badly wanted to start his own company making gunpowder, but he didn't have the business acumen nor the financial backing to begin with. His "pirates" were knowledgeable and would make good employees, but none were adults, and he himself was torn at the thought of having them work at such a young age.

"I told Roy that I would discuss the matter with my father's organization, that perhaps we could form a partnership," Lily said to Hannah, with breakfast going well.

"Did you ever mention the family business by name? Did you ever mention 'L M Hardshore Associates' ?" Hannah asked.

"Come to think of it, no, I did not," Lily replied. "Do you really think Roy and his pirates work in my tin mine?"

"I strongly suspect so," Hannah replied. "Finding the business name on that piece of cloth I showed you was a clue. I have a plan."

Hannah agreed to play billiards with the locals, to find out whatever information she could. Breakfast concluded, and Hannah as "Hank" had to wait until later in the day when more men were available from their shifts. Indeed, Hannah as "Hank" won several such games, forcing several of the locals to be in her debt. She pressed them to pay up, and in the process, she struck a deal to have debts settled in exchange for being let into a local building of her choice, on the sly.

Now tin mining in Cornwall had a history of stannary law, a local legal system that governed mining. And although the Cornish Stannary Parliament ended in 1753, there was still a Stannary Court. By herself, Hannah would have started the investigation by obtaining court records through official means, but of course winning at billiards with the locals has its privileges, and so that is how she ended up in the records building, unofficial-like. The records were stored seemingly haphazardly, so much so that Hannah was convinced she would either suffocate from the moldy air or become lost in the piled heaps of parchment. As it turned out, she did not need to. One of the locals had forewarned her that speedy deals were stored in a broom closet, which she found.

Looking through the closet documents, she saw the true records of Lily's mine. On one such document were names of the workers and their ages—all adults, but on a second document was a list of names and ages with pictorial drawings. These workers were under 18 years of age, and yes, they were Roy and his "pirates".

Hannah returned the documents to the closet and returned to Lily. The two returned to the Hardshore estate and discussed the matter with Carmichael.

"They are governed by stannary law," Carmichael said. "They set their own rules on workers."

"Then we must change that. Force them into new rules," Lily said.

"Even Great Britain cannot enact laws over stannary law. It cannot be done," Carmichael said. "Lily. Your successes in business are astonishing. But politics and law are another matter."

"Why should it be another matter?" Lily pondered. "Tin mines are business. I am in business. I will use my business against theirs. The law will simply have to play catch-up. These men who believe in child labor have created their own rut. They are unable to leave it, much as my father became trapped in his belief that the longbow was forever. It is not. Gunpowder replaced the longbow, and gunpowder will replace child labor. Gunpowder need not be, 'An Invention so inhuman, barbarous and cruel,' as King James said. The very children who work in my mine, Roy and the Gunpowder Pirates, have proven that gunpowder can be tamed for good. They did so for the November 5th celebration, and I believe they can do so for mining."

Carmichael knew that once Lily grabbed hold of an idea, it was useless to talk her out of it. And so, he assisted her in her plan. Lily sent Hannah and other agents to Cornwall to look after Roy and his pirates. Then, Lily issued word that her mine was to cease operations, "temporarily", for "inspection and repair".

The mine was shut down, and before anyone put two and two together, Roy and his pirates were transported to a newly-built trade school for boys in Cornwall that Lily had commissioned. The school was so new that only Marcus, the albino caretaker and bouncer, was in charge. Marcus was excellent at keeping the school secure, but lesson plans did not exist, and so the first few weeks were little more than the various children sharing what they learned with one another. Finding a proper teacher to run the school was another matter, and she had Carmichael look urgently for one.

Meanwhile, the co-owners of Lily's tin mine were furious. They took their case to the Stannary Court, but the Court ruled in Lily's favor since she had a majority stake.

From the court case, Lily learned that a number of underage girls had been used as bal maidens, working on the mine surface to process ore sent up from below. They each worked many days at a time just to earn one penny. Hannah was hurt to find out that she had missed the young bal maidens in her investigation at the records building, but it soon became clear why—they were considered so unimportant as to not even be listed in the secret records.

Lily was determined to find a place in a school for the underage bal maidens. She sent Hannah out to find a proper teacher while Lily had the new school built. Realizing she would now have two schools to staff, Lily decided to send her best millwrights and managers down to the boys' trade school (called Roy's Gunpowder Pirate School) and run it partly as a business and partly as a school. This worked out, as the boys already knew their gunpowder and were soon making machines to produce explosives for mining. Lily ensured that the school educated first and would not devolve into just another child-labor situation.

Education, yes, education. Lily could not emphasize enough how important this was, for it was to be the next advancement in mining. This next advancement was Lily's vision of controlling gunpowder to spare the drudgery of pitting the limits of human strength against the great forces of nature.

While gunpowder could prove useful in conquering nature, it wouldn't be applicable for helping the bal maidens. They needed their own school, with education in both a trade, and how to deal with other matters. They would need a strong teacher. And so, it was with welcome relief that Hannah returned with news of a prospect.

Chapter 14:

The Choices at St. Agnes

The former co-owners of Lily's tin mine fell into financial ruin. Desperate, they sold their portions to L M Hardshore Associates for a fraction of what the mine was worth when in production. Being shut down, however, meant it produced nothing and was worth all but the same amount, and so that was how Lily masterminded such a bargain of a deal.

However, several co-owners were still in debt to others, as they had borrowed heavily to fund their share and had lived extravagant lifestyles upon the backs of the under-trodden workers.

"If we cannot pay, we will be forced into a workhouse!" three of the co-owners agreed in a secret meeting.

The idea of spending their remaining days in a workhouse so rattled their souls that they looked to outside help. And they found it. In a pub in the southwestern tip of Cornwall, the three were told that arrangements could be made. They were asked to step out of the pub into an alley, and they were clubbed over the head.

When they awoke, they were bound to chairs inside a ship that was stranded against the rocks. With each set of waves that crashed against the rocks, the ship shimmied. The room itself was multi-tiered, with steps connecting each.

"I recognize the crashing of the waves by the sound," said one of the ex-owners. "We are in the Isles of Scilly."

"Where is that?" a second ex-owner asked.

"A group of islands west of Cornwall," said the first.

"St. Agnes to be exact," said Damien, now stepping into the area with an assistant. "Welcome to the Haven for Runaways. Runaways of Debt. My apologies for this introduction, but it was necessary. Here."

The assistant handed each of the ex-owners a document.

"Your debts have been paid. In the eyes of Cornwall and Britain, you are free men," Damien said.

The room began filling with water. Damien and the assistant ascended to a higher tier, forcing the ex-owners to endure the cold seawater on their feet.

"But we are still bound," the first ex-owner said. "If we are free in the eyes of Cornwall and Britain, let loose these bonds!"

"You are free in their eyes, not mine," Damien said. "I am Damien DeVille. Both the sea and I make claim to your bondage, until such compensation is made."

Water continued to rise. The ex-owners became nervous.

"Yes, the tide always returns to claim its due," Damien chuckled. "And so, who shall you pay—the sea, or me?"

"Name your terms," said the first ex-owner.

"But let us out of the water first," said the second.

"As soon as you agree to terms with me, I will release you. Until that time, the sea holds your bond. I will give you options, but pick quickly to change bonds over to me."

"Hurry!" said the second ex-owner.

"First choice—sign over property to me," Damien said. "It must be of sufficient value, say, a plot of land or an equivalent number of cattle. Takers?"

"We have none!" the first ex-owner said.

"Very well. Second choice—become a blockade runner for me. You will work on a ship with others to transport goods from France and other unnamed places to wherever I choose. Often you will be required to successfully sail past a British blockade. Death is possible, but at least you will have more time to think about it," Damien said.

"I choose that," the first ex-owner said.

"Wise choice," Damien said as he loosened the bonds of the first ex-owner and allowed him to a safe tier.

The water level was up to the waist of the two remaining ex-owners.

"Quickly! What other options do you offer?" the second ex-owner asked.

"Help recruit slaves for the Barbary pirates," Damien said. "You will become a slave yourself, but instead of working in North Africa, you will stay in the southwest corner of Britain and bring recruits here. You will have a quota to fill, and should you fall short, you will be sent to North Africa yourself to meet the quota. Temporarily. Then you shall return here to find more recruits. If you do not like the sea, this option is recommended."

The seawater had reached upper-torso level.

"I want out of the sea. Out of the sea!" the second ex-owner said. "I choose that one. Unbind me! Please!"

"Excellent choice," Damien said as the assistant helped the second ex-owner from his bonds and onto a safe tier with the first.

The sea level had reached the third ex-owner's neck. Indeed, it occasioned his lips as if to invite the third ex-owner to the depth of drowning in the sea.

"Other options! Please!" the third begged.

"There are no other options," Damien said. "Property, blockade running, or recruitment."

"I am too old for the sea. Too old to recruit. I have no property! Please!" the third begged as he struggled to lift his mouth above the waterline.

"No property? None? Come now. Anything a legal land-owner has in his possession is property. Land? Money? Cattle? People?"

"People are not...are not...property," the third struggled to say.

"Ah, then you do have something. People. Or a person," Damien said. "What do you have? What do you have!"

The third choked on seawater now entering his lungs. He struggled to get air.

"He has a daughter," the first ex-owner offered. "About seventeen years of age."

Damien's eyes lit up.

"A daughter. Well! Is this true? Do you have a daughter?" Damien asked the third.

"Yes," the third struggled to say. "But I...I..."

"He agrees to give his daughter to you," the first ex-owner said.

"I..." the third continued. He had meant to say, "I do not give my daughter," but the seawater finally caught his lungs, and he fell unconscious.

"I accept your daughter," Damien said as the assistant loosened the third's bonds, pulled him to a safe tier, and forced water from his lungs to encourage a return to life.

The third ex-owner did return to life.

"Congratulations," Damien said. "You have the best choice of all. You will live a normal life free of danger. No risk of dying at the hands of a British blockade ship, and no risk of perpetual servitude for the Barbary pirates. Again, congratulations."

The first two ex-owners were sent on their assignments. The third went home—accompanied by Damien's assistant.

"Ruth," the third ex-owner said to his daughter.

"Father? Who is this?" Ruth asked.

"This is..." the father started to say.

"You have been promised in marriage to Damien DeVille, a man of means and 63 years of age," the assistant said.

"Father!" Ruth protested.

"This was not my—" the father started to say, but the assistant clubbed him senseless, and he fell to the floor.

"Father!" Ruth's voice echoed as she was driven away by cart.

Chapter 15:

Haven for Runaways

Lily and Hannah as "Hank" arrived in a small coal-mining town in Devonshire as dusk approached. It was the town where Hannah had met the prospective teacher for Lily's new school. The town was small, with several huts and shanties lining the area.

"These are shops," Hannah said to Lily's surprise.

"Such dilapidation," Lily said. "To see people living in squalor."

"It's this one. 'Mining Lights and Tidbits. Gloria Frankenmuth, Sole Proprietor'," Hannah read.

Hannah knocked on the door.

"No answer," Lily said. "Look, there's a note on the door, 'No longer in business'."

"Gloria Frankenmuth. Yes, that's her. Strange. She was in business a few days ago. Let's go around back," Hannah said.

The two walked around back to an alley between two rows of these huts and shanties. The two were careful to step around the muck of refuse. Dust coatings on strewn debris above and below left everything dark and dingy. Lily and Hannah heard a voice partway down. They could not see who made the voice, but a flicker of light suggested where they might go. The two ventured forth.

"At the top of this hill is a group of rocks, where the Fairy Princess of Wayward Bees does dwell," the voice said, followed by the shushing of excited children.

Lily and Hannah reached the light and the voice but managed to stay in the darkness to avoid detection. Hannah nodded to Lily and pointed to the speaker, that this was Gloria Frankenmuth. And it was. Gloria sat on a wooden crate with a circle of seven children sitting around her. She and the children had darkened complexions from long-term exposure to coal dust. It was as if their skin needed deep cleaning for pores desperately in need of relief. But no such relief at the moment.

Gloria had her back to a shanty and had another crate to her right, atop which sat a skep of bees, with the skep woven of soft rush. This particular one had two parts—a larger lower half and a smaller upper half. The skep was somewhat fashioned like a snowman, with sticks for arms, coal for eyes and a nose, a thin metal bowl for a hat, and a thin strip of tattered material for a scarf. A bee entrance was at its base. Atop the hat was a lit beeswax candle, holding a steady flame and releasing a pleasant aroma that cleansed the surrounding air.

"She calls out to lost bees like this," Gloria said, letting out a soft, wispy trill.

From above came a bee. It hovered around the skep, not sure of where to go. Gloria produced a length of rush from the inside of her cloak, touched it to the flame, watched it alight, and then blew out its own flame, allowing a line of smoke to drift upward from the rush. She extended the rush out to the wayward bee and used the smoke as a call.

"Follow the smoke, little bee," she said as she led the bee to the bee entrance.

The bee followed, lit on the lower side of the skep near the entrance, walked toward the entrance, and went in.

"Fairy Princess of Wayward Bees uses her rushlights to signal runaway bees from afar. They fly away from beekeepers who only keep them alive long enough to make a little honey. Who wants to signal a wayward bee?" Gloria asked the children.

All children raised their hands, excited.

"Hold your fists out," she said. "Now I'll count."

Gloria held out the still-smoldering rush stick and pointed at each child's fist in turn as she said:

> *Little bee, little bee*
> *In the air*
> *How many people*
> *Can you scare?*

Gloria's rush pointer stopped at one child who said, "Seven."

"Ess Eee Vee Eee Enn makes 'seven' and out you go," Gloria said.

With, "go," Gloria pointed to the fist that had to be retracted by the child, who did. Gloria then went on with another verse:

> *Little bee, little bee*
> *In the sky*
> *How many hours*
> *Can you fly?*

Gloria repeated as before, with a child selecting a number, and Gloria spelling out the number to eliminate another fist. Gloria had other verses too:

Little bee, little bee
By the lake
How many flowers
Do you shake?

The "Little bee" verses had many variations: by the tree, by the ocean, near the road, and so on. Finally the time had come, where only two children had fists still out. One child was eliminated, and the other won. Gloria lit her rush stick and handed it to the child. The rush light shone brilliantly to the children's delight, and the child with the light walked in the area, only to shriek in fright at the discovery of "Hank" and Lily.

"It's a man and a woman," the child said.

"I am Hank, and this is Lily Hardshore," Hannah said.

"Welcome, fellow friends," Gloria said. "Won't you come over?"

"We would like to purchase candles," Lily said.

"My store is closed," Gloria said. "But you're welcome to a rush light. I will give you a special one from my skep."

Gloria tapped the side of the skep, which was woven from soft rush (remember?). A stem stuck out, and she gently pulled it out. The skep seemed to heal itself, reshaping and reforming itself to close the gap. The children were in awe at the sight.

"Be kind to your bees, and they will tend to the soft rush, like gardeners of the fields, for this is a living skep, with the rush grown and tended to by the bees, filling their wax in the rush. But one should not be greedy and take all rush at once. Bees need time to regrow new ones," Gloria explained to the children as she handed the rush length to Lily.

"I would like to light the rush, but I have no tinderbox," Lily said.

"Here!" the child with the rush light offered as she held her flame close to Lily.

Lily lit her rush light and smiled. Without warning, the children rushed off, scattering as if to avoid being caught doing something not allowed. Lily, Hannah, and Gloria then were left behind.

"They aren't supposed to be around me," Gloria explained.

"Gloria Frankenmuth, this is Lily Hardshore. Lily, this is Gloria," Hannah said.

The two exchanged greetings.

"Your store said it was closed," Hannah said. "You were in business last we met."

"Times have been unfriendly," Gloria said. "My husband died in the mines, I have no children of my own, and my business has failed. I have but this bee hive and a small audience of children. But that is all."

Lily took a hard look at Gloria. Yes, her complexion seemed perpetually dirty, her clothes were badly tired, and she had tired lines of long days and little to eat.

"I was a teacher once. Before all this," Gloria said. "Children deserve the richness of learning, not the poverty of the daily grind. I..."

"Is there anything keeping you here? Any oath or duty?" Lily asked.

"Nothing," Gloria said. "Even at my end, I spend my last morsels teaching the children, if even just a little."

"Please be my guest at my place," Lily said. "I will give you a good meal and a place to clean up. Dust this town's coal off your feet."

"I take no charity," Gloria said.

"It is no charity," Lily said. "I have need for a teacher. I'm building a new school for girls in Devonshire, and I need someone familiar with the area. This is no charity. It is a business meeting. But I cannot conduct a proper meeting in this venue."

Gloria agreed to come with them. She gathered up her skep and rode in the back of Lily's carriage. Hannah drove, of course, and Lily sat next to Hannah, but Lily often turned back to speak with Gloria. Lily wanted to know more about Gloria, but with the day nearly spent and Gloria showing her fatigue, Lily realized that her questions would have to wait. Lily arranged for the three to stay at an inn for the night, where Gloria could be well-fed and well-rested for the next day.

The next day came. Despite having a good meal the prior night at the inn and having a strong bath, the coal dinginess on Gloria's skin would not come out. Hannah loaned Gloria a fresh set of clothes along with glove, scarf, and a hat that heavily obscured Gloria's face, so at least Gloria would not be ashamed to be seen. They arrived at the Hardshore estate, and there they held discussion.

Gloria explained her prior teaching experience, that she gave everything she could to the children, but other teachers did not have such loving methods and instead spent more classroom time with tortuous discipline such as staring at a row of letters on a board instead of useful education. The headmaster supported such methods, claiming children were destined for the Devil unless they were steered in the "proper" direction. And so, the children begged their parents to work in the mines, as that was less drudgery than the school itself. The parents agreed, and the school closed due to lack of students. Though Gloria fought for classroom reform at the time, her words fell on deaf ears, and so she sought to help these children even after they went to the mines. Her husband got a mining job in the same town as these children, but her husband died in a mining accident, she sold things in a store as long as she could, but she wasn't much of a business person, feeling too guilty of gluttony to charge a proper price, and giving away more things than she should have on seeing the plight of others. And the coal dust. Oh! It was everywhere. She felt like some sort of under-trodden chimney sweep and didn't have the confidence to venture to other schools to find work. Her only companion through everything turned out to be the bee hive skep.

"Yes, I was quite taken by that," Lily said.

Gloria explained that as her store business failed, she went on long walks in the countryside. She discovered that some beekeepers were still using the old wicker skep, that they would start a hive and after a time would roast the skeps over burning sulfur to kill the bees for whatever meager beeswax and honey might be inside. Gloria found that those few bees who escaped such a death went to her—not to sting but for escape. She took two disused skeps that had not turned out fruitful and remade them into the configuration she now had, with upper part being for beeswax and honey only. She discovered a collection of special soft rush plants that she could use to piece the skep together, a kind that the bees took to and entered into a symbiotic relationship with, each receiving benefit from the other. Gloria then showed how she could light a rush stem briefly, blow it out, and use the smoke to send any bees from the dome back to the base so that she could close off the two and remove the dome.

"See? A little beeswax and honey," she said. "But the hive survives."

"The hive survives," Lily said.

"So would the school," Hannah added.

"If I were to run a school," Gloria mused, "I would start out with morning instruction, explaining what to look for during project time and what questions to pursue, followed by project time with the bees and perhaps even weaving for making rush wicker things, then follow up with afternoon instruction to answer questions and see how things were the same or different. I would then announce what to look forward to for the next day so that my students would become eager for that next day and think about things."

Lily and Hannah exchanged glances of exuberance.

"You would make an excellent headmistress," Lily said. "I wish to hire you immediately."

"But I have nothing prepared yet. No books, no lesson plans, nothing," Gloria said.

"Not even a school built yet," Hannah added (who of course was not posing as Hank and had in fact let Gloria in on the secret early in their meeting).

"You can start here, on the estate," Lily said. "I will give you what you need, including safe harbor for the bees. I have a few children of workers who need a place to go during the day as it is. You can start with them in one of the barns. It isn't much, but it will give us both time to prepare for the school."

"And I'll help wash out that coal dust," Hannah said. "I have a special cleaner I use for such things. Works well for mud on horses too."

Lily and Gloria laughed.

"I hope I can do better than horse soap," Gloria said.

"I think you will," Lily said. "You can add it as part of the school curriculum, making things to undo things like coal dust."

It was settled then. Gloria would head up the new school. A barn was quickly converted into a temporary school and project shop. Lily had suppliers and workers give Gloria whatever she needed. It wasn't long before Gloria had multiple wooden bee hives with easily removed beeswax and honey. These two ingredients were easily refined for a variety of products from beeswax candles to salve, shampoo, antimicrobials, and foodstuffs. Lily had one of her business associates handle the financial management of things. Though Gloria wasn't truly in a business situation at the moment, Lily made sure Gloria acted as if she were, understanding cost of supplies, efficiency of labor, and value of product produced. Gloria made out her lesson plans and had a working school of girls going.

Gloria's plan worked well. The girls quickly learned English, math, science, and business—all while incorporating this knowledge with bee tending, rush weaving, and flowers. Yes, flowers. Gloria discovered that although the bees went afar to get nectar, growing flowers locally for the bees to visit gave Gloria a more precise method of giving instruction to the bees, specifically in how the flowers were grown, what fertilizers were used, and how the plants were grafted and mixed.

The new school was built very quickly, and the day came for Gloria and her bees to move. To Gloria's surprise, some of her older students had been so inspired by Gloria's teaching style that they had been studying teaching on the side, and so when Gloria was about to move to the new school, these girls offered to go with her—as teachers under her leadership. A few tears later, and Gloria with her teaching staff was underway. Lily ensured enough helpers carried all needed supplies, the bee hives, and the flowers with care.

One last surprise—on reaching the new school, Gloria was surprised to see a welcoming committee with Hannah as "Hank" and Lily attending. The school itself was named, "Gloria Frankenmuth School for Girls".

Gloria could barely speak. But her overwhelmed emotions quickly settled, and she gave out orders with the proper confidence of a rightful headmistress. One more thing. Her complexion had completely cleared by now, thanks to the specially refined beeswax and honey lotion her school had made. All were cheerful to see Gloria in such spirits and energy, and so the school had a wonderful start.

In fact, things did so well that Lily and Hannah were no longer needed for help. Gloria took full control, seeking out wayward girls and pulling them into the school, where they earned their board and keep with bee, wicker, and flower projects.

It wasn't long before Gloria sent the bees out to find poor hives in danger of being exterminated by sulfur or other means. Her bees invited the other bees out of their hives into proper hives at Gloria's school. In some ways, the situation was analogous to Lily's way of closing down the Cornwall tin mine to stop child labor. But Gloria had a slightly different method of dealing with the beekeepers. Instead of shutting them all down cold and leaving them angry and bitter, she sent messages to them that her bees had found them out, and they had better improve their beekeeping with non-deadly wooden hives or else their bees would leave.

Some beekeepers laughed at her proposal. But it wasn't long before the first few beekeepers learned the hard way that Gloria was correct, and so most beekeepers improved their hives and were able to keep their bees. Better yet, by keeping their bees alive, they were able to improve their own productivity.

Yes, Gloria could have been ruthless and simply forced these other beekeepers out of business and thus expand her business quickly. But she had a soft heart and was more interested in the care and instruction of her students. Word got back to Lily, and though Lily would have been more aggressive as mentioned, she did not object to Gloria, as Lily's main objective of giving girls a better education and life was also met, and so there were no disagreements between Gloria and Lily.

It came upon a time that Gloria's bees discovered first one and then another runaway girl. Gloria had an elaborate communication system with these bees, with Gloria sending instruction through flowers, and bees doing a variety of special communication dances on tables to reply back (in fact, Gloria's students took special classes for communicating with the bees, and so they could do the work of sending and receiving messages for Gloria so that Gloria could manage other things). Word got back to Lily, who was concerned that so many girls were running away from things. These girls were often found hiding in obscure places in barns or under buildings—places adults would not think to check but places the bees were able to check on by squeezing through cracks in the boards.

"Many have escaped from mines, some from abusive homes, and one from a promised marriage," Gloria explained on one of her business visits to the Hardshore estate with Lily and Hannah.

Lily was especially disconcerted to hear about a girl running away to avoid being forced into a marriage.

"Her name is Ruth," Gloria said. "I brought her along."

Ruth was walked in, but the girl was so terribly distraught that her eyes looked straight ahead, and she gave no reaction to the environment around her.

"The other girls were thankful to join the school," Gloria said. "But none have been as traumatized as Ruth here. Her name was all I could get out of her."

"Hannah," Lily said. "This is beyond my skill."

"I will take her among the animals. See how she does with them. Basic care and interaction," Hannah said.

"Please do. I hope for her return to health," Lily said.

In the days that followed, Ruth did come out of her shell and speak. She revealed the reason she ran away, to avoid becoming the unwilling bride of a much older man. After spending time with the animals, Ruth took a liking first to servicing the horses' hooves, and then to masonry jobs around the stables. She was so enamored with masonry that even the local masons were impressed with her work and wanted to hire her right away. But Ruth was more than just one who piled stone to form a building. She learned to cut stone in such precise ways as to not need lime mortar.

Ruth's anxiety did not fully abate. She felt vulnerable in the open air, as if men from afar would suddenly whisk her away by horseback. Even when riding a horse herself, she could not shake the feeling. She preferred then to work inside. After a short time, Hannah gave her report to Lily.

"I have done all I can for her. She still fears the outside. I suggest we send her back to Gloria to see what extra help she can provide," Hannah said.

Lily agreed. Ruth was willing too. Lily allowed Ruth to pick her own horse and keep it, which Ruth used to ride down to the Gloria Frankenmuth School for Girls. Hannah accompanied Ruth and bade her good luck before Hannah returned to the Hardshore estate.

Ruth was instructed on the ways of the bees, how to send them messages with flowers and how to read their dances. But as it was, Ruth ended up making little stone implements for the bee products—stone containers for beeswax and for beeswax lotions, stone candle holders for the beeswax candles, stone jars for honey, and so on. With the help of the other students, Ruth came up with a portable lantern running on beeswax that doubled as a one-burner stove. She looked to improve the device, but all concluded that beeswax as a fuel wasn't enough. Something else was needed.

One day when Lily and Hannah visited Gloria's school, a meeting was held with Ruth and Gloria to decide how best to continue Ruth's progress, as Ruth still was afraid of the open outdoors. It was agreed that given Ruth's masonry skills and especially with the lantern, she would visit Roy's Gunpowder Pirate School on a joint effort for using Ruth's lantern in mining. But Ruth would not go alone. She wanted assistance.

And so, Hannah as "Hank" went with Ruth, along with one of Gloria's teachers (Tess) who was well trained in communicating with the bees. They took a portable skep with base hive and dome for honey and beeswax, as per normal design. There was also a quick-release latch for allowing the bees easy access to the outdoors if needed.

"Keep a small swarm flying above and ahead, to scout for danger," Gloria urged as the group left Devonshire for Cornwall, and yes, with a small swarm of bees scouting up and ahead, though at least they were friendly to Ruth and her cause.

Chapter 16:

Roy and Ruth

Hannah, Ruth, and Tess reached Roy's Gunpowder Pirate School but were surprised and saddened to see that a small portion of the school wall had fallen into rubble. Ruth rushed up to help search the debris for survivors before Hannah and Tess could say anything.

"How is it the bees did not warn us?" Hannah asked Tess.

"The bees did not sense danger from people," Tess said. "This was no attack."

"No, it wasn't," Roy said, walking up to Hannah and Tess. "At least not in the conventional sense. A bad mixture of lime gave way. I am Roy Finchley. Hank I already know."

"I am Tess, a teacher from Gloria Frankenmuth School for Girls," Tess said.

"A new school Lily and I helped start in Devonshire," Hannah as "Hank" said. "They specialize in beehives and can talk to the bees."

"I do not doubt your words about this not being an attack," Tess said to Roy. "But I wish to send out my bees to check, to be sure. Do not worry. They will not sting."

"As you wish," Roy said. "But I must confess that although we are excellent at making gunpowder, our skills in masonry are still developing."

Tess released the bees. They hovered upward, high up in fact, and then suddenly they flew off toward the west.

"They are onto a scented trail," Tess said. "They will be gone for a time. Let us go help."

Tess and Hannah went to help clean up the destroyed section of the school. Roy went after them.

"I should not allow you to help," Roy said. "It could be dangerous."

"And yet you are," Hannah said.

"I noticed that too," Tess said. "Your expression changed the moment you saw Ruth."

Hannah and Tess laughed.

"It...I...it is just I am not used to seeing...seeing..." Roy stumbled.

"Go on. Go help her," Hannah said to Roy as she and Tess continued to laugh.

Hannah and Tess watched as Roy thanked Hannah for "permission" to speak with Ruth. As it turned out, Roy and Ruth spent more time speaking with each other and exchanging pleasantries than anything else. Ruth pointed out how parts of the school could have been built better and used her masonry expertise to detail as much. Roy did much listening and at times looked around as if wondering why he never hired proper masons to build his school strong enough to prevent such destruction from blasts. Meanwhile, the bees returned and landed on a slab of rock a fair distance from the school. Hannah and Tess ran over to them.

"They are dancing," Tess said as she and Hannah reached the slab.

"What do they say?" Hannah asked.

"They confirm that no one attacked this school," Tess said. "But the explosion and smoke has attracted attention. A group of men is heading this way from the western shore."

"Friendly or foe?" Hannah asked.

"I do not know," Tess said.

"Roy is well defended here," Hannah mused. "This group of men would not be after him."

"Could they be after us?" Tess asked.

"Barbary pirates have kidnapped people before. Then there is Ruth. She is a runaway," Hannah said.

"So are many of our students at Gloria's school," Tess said.

"Whoever these men are, they must not know about these runaways," Hannah said. "They might employ underhanded methods to take them."

"I will send the bees back out," Tess said.

Tess took several dried flowers and a small container with a liquid from the inside of her cloak. She crushed the flowers in a particular sequence and sprinkled the liquid on the slab. The bees danced over the liquid and then flew off.

"Let's check on Ruth," Tess said. "We should not leave her unchaperoned."

"Are you afraid of the Barbary pirates?" Hannah asked.

"I hope we'll not have need for such fear," Tess said.

The two returned to the destroyed part of the school, but neither Roy nor Ruth were there. The two walked around further, but still no luck. A few bees still remained in Tess's special skep, which she carried with her, and so she sent them out to look for Ruth. They hovered high in the air for a moment before suddenly darting away from the school toward a small stone building.

"They are going for that little church over there," Tess said.

"Yes, they are," Hannah said as the two walked that way.

"Is Roy a religious man?" Tess asked.

"Not when I last saw him," Hannah said.

The two reached the church and entered in time to see Roy and Ruth exchanging vows to a minister.

"Stop!" Hannah shouted.

"Too late. We are married," Ruth said as she and Roy turned around.

"Apparently we were afraid of the wrong pirates," Tess said.

"Yes. Not the Barbary but the Gunpowder Pirates," Hannah said. "Roy, I'm disappointed in you."

"We had to get married," Ruth said. "We realized we were soulmates from the very beginning."

"Yes, we are madly in love," Roy said.

"The marriage is legal and binding," the minister said.

"With no witnesses?" Hannah pointed out.

The bees Tess had sent out emerged from a spot in the church ceiling, danced briefly on a marriage document, and then returned to Tess's skep.

"They are my witnesses!" Ruth grinned.

"Oh, Gloria will become aside herself when she hears of this," Tess said.

"Lily too. We promised to protect Ruth," Hannah said.

"I will protect Ruth," Roy said. "And I still have my Gunpowder Pirates to back me."

"Something doesn't sit right with this. So sudden," Hannah said.

Hannah motioned Tess to follow her outside the church while Roy and Ruth discussed their new life together.

"I think Ruth got married for another reason," Hannah said. "She ran away from her father to avoid being forced into an unwanted marriage."

"And by marrying Roy, that is no longer possible," Tess added. "At least not legally."

"Then we must be wary of the illegal," Hannah said. "If her father is one of those approaching men...hmm. Tess, is there a way to tell if one of those men *is* Ruth's father?"

"Bees have an acute sense of smell," Tess said. "I could have them look for anyone with the same familial scent as Ruth."

Hannah nodded to proceed, and Tess nodded back. Tess re-sent out her little group of bees that had witnessed Ruth's wedding (who still remembered Ruth's scent). Their mission was to find anyone related to her, starting with the group of men that the main set of bees were observing.

"They will search," Tess said.

Hannah and Tess heard music coming from the school.

"Strange," Tess said. "I did not know that these boys use music to produce gunpowder."

"They do not," Hannah said. "Anything from the bees?"

"Nothing," Tess said. "I'll leave the skep out here in case they return. Let's follow the music."

Hannah and Tess did that. They reached the building with music, entered, and found quite a reception party underway for Roy's and Ruth's marriage. Occasional mini-fireworks were set off in celebration. Hannah and Tess shrugged their shoulders before joining the festivities.

After a time, Marcus walked in.

"Your bees have returned," he said to Tess.

"I will check," Tess said to Hannah before going outside with Marcus.

"I did not wish to alert the others," Marcus said to Tess once the two were outside and alone. "But I caught the minister with several bee stings. From your bees. It is concerning. We do not wish our people here to be stung by your bees. If there are more cases—"

"Thank you, Marcus. Let's see what the bees have to say."

Tess watched as the bees danced on a table.

"The group of men is gone," Tess said. "It is as if they have left these shores."

"Perhaps they have," Marcus said.

"The bees who stung the minister have spoken as well. They say the minister is a spy for these men, that he is not a minister at all," Tess said.

"A spy. Do they say what kind?" Marcus asked.

"No," Tess said. "They have no additional information."

"I will find out what kind of spy he is," Marcus said. "These boys have worked too hard to see their secrets of gunpowder stolen."

Marcus departed. After a moment, Hannah approached. Tess told her about the disappearance of the men and the minister's deceit.

"The marriage is not valid," Tess said.

"Roy and Ruth believe it to be valid. I must warn them," Hannah said.

"Wait," Tess said. "Someone approaches."

"It is only I," Marcus said. "I have the 'minister'."

Marcus forced the minister to explain who he was. Yes, he was no minister, and the marriage was a ruse to gain time and information. The minister was a spy for Damien DeVille, and yes, he was after the gunpowder technique. He was also a scout for prospective slaves for the Barbary pirates. The minister had heard of Ruth being in Devonshire and had sent word of her presence there at the Gloria Frankenmuth School for Girls. The pirates decided to change plans and go after Ruth first before plundering the gunpowder school, thus their withdrawal to the sea to then sneak into Devonshire. But the arrival of Ruth was an unexpected event. The minister had meant to send word of her arrival when bees stung him.

"Ruth is here in Cornwall!" the minister yelled as if hoping to be heard by the pirates. "In Cornwall!"

Marcus clunked the minister on the head. The minister fell silent.

"We must warn Gloria. We must go to her school," Tess said.

"I will go," Marcus said. "And I shall bring this *minister* with me to ensure his good behavior. We will prepare for attack."

"Attack?" Hannah said. "Did they say when?"

"I do not know," the minister said. "My messenger crow has not yet arrived...until now!"

The minister's crow perched on his shoulder. The minister untied a message from its leg, but Marcus grabbed the message before the minister could.

"The message confirms the planned attack on Gloria Frankenmuth's school. It does not say when," Marcus said. "If only this bird could scout out for us."

"That it will never do, no matter what torture you may inflict upon me," the minister said.

"We don't need the bird. My bees can do the scouting," Tess said. "I will go with you, Marcus."

"Bedevil you and your bees!" the minister spat, but Marcus twisted the minister's arm again.

"Well? Are you coming too?" Marcus said to Hannah.

"No, I will stay behind," Hannah said. "Someone must stay behind and watch after Ruth. They still must be warned of things."

It was agreed. Hannah stayed behind and bade farewell to Tess, Marcus, and the minister.

Chapter 17:

The Siege

When Marcus, Tess, the bees, the minister, and his bird arrived at Gloria's school, they were happy to see that Lily was still there. Marcus and Tess told Gloria and Lily all that had happened. Both Gloria and Lily were dismayed to hear about Ruth's wedding but relieved when they learned it was not valid. Lily promised to support Ruth for a proper wedding when the time was right, but all agreed that the time was not now. Just as the discussion was complete, Tess's bees arrived. They danced, and she read their message.

"The group of men has reached the coast by ship," Tess said aloud.

The crow flew off.

"Stop that bird!" Lily shouted.

Tess sent her bees after the bird, but the bird was too fast and got away.

"If only we had archers," Tess said.

"I do not trust these men," Gloria said. "We must make plans to protect the school."

"Marcus and Tess, stay here and protect the school," Lily said. "I will ride off and seek aid."

Though Hannah usually took Lily around by carriage, Lily had been quietly learning to ride horses with speed and surety. She borrowed one of Gloria's quickest steeds and rode off.

The crow reached the men. They were Barbary pirates, led by Ruth's father.

"You know the deal," Ruth's father said. "You may take all for slaves at the school where Ruth has been hiding. You will then begin your campaign to find Ruth and send her to Damien as my payment to him."

"We will take our share of slaves first," the lead pirate said. "They will make for good bargaining chips for your daughter Ruth. We will wait for darkness."

Darkness came, but Lily had not yet returned. Gloria closed classes for the day and had the girls take a defensive position with anything they could swing as a weapon, but inside the school walls. The school itself had been somewhat built like a castle with a perimeter wall (but no moat), and so one could not so easily walk in once the perimeter doors were closed, which they were. The group of men grew close, but they halted behind a group of rocks a bit more than a stone's throw away.

"Send in the crow," the lead pirate said.

"I don't know why you wait here when you could storm right through," Ruth's father grumbled.

"Stealth is an art form best practiced for such occasions," the lead pirate said. "A thief in the night is undetected until he is long departed and beyond reach."

The crow flew to the perimeter, noted how things were closed up, and returned to the pirates. And as it did, bees already perched on the perimeter wall noted the crow and then returned to Tess—all unobserved by the crow.

"They are here," Tess reported to the others.

"I will man the main gate," Marcus said.

Marcus went to the main gate door and watched. A lone man approached. It was Ruth's father, but he passed himself off as just a common passerby.

"Greetings! My name is Peter Petalby," Ruth's father said, giving out his true name. "I bring tidings of good cheer from the Crown," not true, "and I bring offers of aid to those who are ill," also not true. "May I enter and take census of your sickly? The Crown is eager to help. Have you been ill long?"

"I am well," Marcus replied. "We are all well."

"How is your wife?" Peter asked.

"She is well," Marcus said.

"I see," Peter continued. "How is her family?"

"They are well," Marcus said.

"I see that too," Peter said. "Look. Let me show you something."

Peter pulled out a document from his cloak and handed it to Marcus.

"Why should I spend time looking at this?" Marcus said. "Are you some sort of common peddler?"

"It is a job offer for me," Peter said. "An offer in Persia."

"I thought you were here to check on our health," Marcus said, becoming very suspicious.

"Persia, the cradle of civilization," Peter said, pushing this false story onto Marcus. "Great opportunities await those who wish to go. Opportunities and riches. I could take you there. This place is no good for you. Schools are closing like the plague. Children are going into industry. These schools are only a temporary death. You want life, don't you? Life and a future? A man of your size and talent could do far better than a place like this. But no, you will stay. And I will be the smarter one, won't I? The smarts of Peter Petalby are difficult to catch, but then I did not catch you sooner in life. I feel badly for your years lost to the lesser. They only serve to drag you down. Persia, my friend. Persia!"

"Take your business elsewhere," Marcus said.

"What. What is going on with you, my friend? You are in a place of despair. Such tones of anger and dismissal. I offer help in the humblest of ways. But I see your need is deeper than we anticipated. The Crown will send people after I go. They will take you to a workhouse, yes, to help build up confidence, confidence that your father never gave you. But you will gain it. I promise you that, sir. Now about the others. How many souls may I inquire are here?"

"You may not inquire at all," Marcus said.

"It is merely a question," Peter continued. "There is no harm in a question. No one goes hungry. No one dies of disease. Please sir, how many are in need of aid? And do not worry, illness comes in all forms. Even a mild fatigue at the end of the day deserves serious consideration. I have lost many friends to such disease. We must be prepared for such circumstances. Do not let darkness creep into your vision, friend. Do not allow your soul to slip into dark places. It happens all but as easily as the rain muddies a clear lake. It happens as the morning dawn becomes troubled by the storms of the day. I am patient, friend. I will wait here by the door as you take your count. Please. Do not be rushed in your count. And let others know I am here. Many such people may find hospitality in their heart. I do hope you find it in yours."

Marcus exerted great patience with Peter's act. To the downtrodden, Peter's words might deceive them into willful obedience. But Marcus had many prior jobs as a bouncer, sending smiths of deception on their faces as he tossed them out of tavern after tavern. Marcus surmised that Peter was not only trying to gain Marcus's confidence, but also to stall for time as the pirates snuck up to strategic positions. Using the crow, they were able to find parts in the wall that were not directly observable by Marcus nor from main windows of the school itself. They prepared to scale it.

What they did not know was that Tess's bees were observing. And not just hers. Other bees from other teachers were also watching. They watched for a few seconds, flew back to dance the message, and then flew back out. In this way, Gloria and her top teachers received real-time progress information on the pirates, as the bees now made it evident that they were.

"Now as it turns out," Peter continued, "one of your ill is a special carrier of disease that can become quite deadly. She should be treated first. Her name is Ruth. You should bring her out first."

"This is the Gloria Frankenmuth School for Girls," Marcus said. "You will not take anyone off these grounds. Go away, now. Go away!"

Peter was not happy at being turned away. He had hoped to trick Marcus and the school for a peaceful way to resolve his little matter of Ruth being sent to Damien and so on, but since Marcus would not budge from his position, it became clear what had to be done. Peter signaled to the pirates, and they launched their attack. They scaled the walls and pulled out their swords. They worked to break down doors, but Marcus ran back to head them off. He too had a sword and began fencing them back. Pirate health held no sway over Marcus, and he heavily injured many to take them out of the fight.

The teachers released their bees, and they swarmed in to attack. Additional pirates were taken out, but some merely covered themselves with more clothing, and so the bees could not reach their skin.

The pirates entered the dormitory chamber. Behind the doors were muffled cries, as if the girls were desperate to hide their fright. The pirates broke down one of the doors. A single candle shone from a central table. Under beds were blankets with slight movement.

"There," said one pirate.

"Girls," smirked another.

The pirates removed part of their clothing to embrace the girls. They pulled at the blankets with speed so as to choose girls of their liking. Instead, they were met with hordes of wasps that had been hidden in special nests that had made the muffled cries.

The wasps took no mercy on their victims, stinging as many pirates as they could. These pirates ran from the building, jumped over the perimeter wall, and headed for the sea.

Other pirates, seeing this deception, kept themselves covered and raced around to the other rooms as quickly as they could. But extra-slippery beeswax had been wiped on the floors, causing these pirates to slip, fall, and often knock themselves unconscious.

Still other pirates came and found that buckets of extra-thick honey fell suddenly on them, causing them to stick in place like flies in a web.

Pirates ran down a particular hallway. Girls pulled ropes made of bee silk, tripped the pirates, and had bees tie up the pirates. In fact, bees used this silk to tie up other pirates as well. But there was one group yet to be dealt with. They remained outside the perimeter wall at the main doors. Peter was with them, and they prepared for a direct assault. Peter shouted to the school using a blowhorn.

"We gave you peaceful discourse, and you ignored us. We gave you quiet surprise, and you deceived us. Now we show our might and muscle. We will break your building to the ground!"

The pirates rolled up a cannon and fired at the main perimeter doors. The cannon ball blasted through clean yet the doors held closed. The cannon was prepared, and another shot was fired. The wall doors burst open. The pirates flooded in, but Marcus had been waiting for them and fired flintlock after flintlock at them from a collection specially prepared for such an invasion. Pirates fell. Others continued to flood in, and they were met with wasps. Still, they did not care and rushed in. Ruth's father was particularly eager to see if his daughter was there and if so, he would drag her out of the siege and take her to Damien directly.

Pirates fired back, as they had flintlocks as well. Bees provided a cloud of cover so that Marcus's position could not be seen, and he escaped the hail of bullets.

It wasn't over. The pirates were forced back by flaming arrows fired from the school. These arrows were coated in sticky beeswax that tended to drip fire upon whatever it landed on. And they did, onto pirates, but not all of them, and so the pirates still surged forward. The school was a bit on a hill, which helped with the next defensive act. Carts of beeswax-coated straw were lit and pushed down the hill from both flanks, catching this surge of pirates. It slowed them, but some still got through. Marcus reappeared at the school doorway, but the push of pirates trampled him. These pirates were so determined that they managed to get into the school and find Gloria Frankenmuth.

Happy with their conquest, they pulled her to the front door and paused. Peter Petalby yelled with his blowhorn.

"We have conquered your school. Surrender now, and there will be no further violence. There need not be bloodshed. Ruth, are you here? Ruth!"

"There need not be bloodshed," Gloria replied in equal volume. "Go back to the sea."

Peter and the pirates laughed.

"Go back to the sea where you belong!" she called again.

With that, what everyone thought were bell towers were in fact water towers. They were released suddenly, and water flooded out at incredible speed. But this wasn't ordinary water. It was especially laced to chemically react with male chemistry and thus sting all those who were male. Marcus, strangely enough, was somewhat protected by his albinism, but the pirates themselves were carried out of the inner perimeter to the outside, into a trough, and out to sea. Gloria herself was nearly swept up in the wash, but Marcus caught her and pulled her to safety.

The pirates were defeated and washed away. Within moments, Lily arrived with Hannah, Roy, Ruth, and the Gunpowder Pirates.

"I doubled back to Cornwall and brought aid," Lily said. "But I see we are too late."

"No, not too late," Gloria said, and she collapsed in total exhaustion.

"We need the help," Marcus said as Hannah and Ruth helped Gloria. "We have depleted our defenses and are vulnerable should they return."

"I will help you there," Roy said. "I will have my boys guard the school. But fire-and-pain does this water sting!"

"Do not drink the water," Marcus said. "And do not touch it, if possible. We will explain all."

The Gunpowder Pirates helped with the cleanup. As it turned out, many new friendships between Gloria's girls and Roy's boys were formed. Ruth was devastated to see her school so badly damaged but relieved to learn that though many girls were injured, all had been spared death.

Chapter 18:

Respite and Reflection

In the days that followed, the Gloria Frankenmuth School for Girls was quickly restored and redecorated. The wasps, unfortunately, were all lost, but several bee hives survived and so that part of the school was not lost.

A new building was built outside the perimeter that also contained a lookout tower to provide additional warning and support against any future attacks. But nearby towns heard of what happened and offered their support as well, and so no further attacks transpired.

A church was built farther up the hill next to an ancient stone circle. The stone circle was used for outdoor ceremonies. The first was the funeral of Peter Petalby. His body washed ashore shortly after the siege, and though intact, it was waterlogged nearly beyond recognition. Ruth was terribly inconsolable, but with the help of Roy and others, she mustered enough strength to go through with the ceremony.

However, all was not for sadness. Lily found a proper minister, surprisingly enough, and she (along with Gloria and the others) approved of Roy and Ruth getting married. They did, and it was a more fulfilling wedding now that Ruth didn't feel compelled to marry to avoid Damien DeVille. She also felt the blessings of the girls' school and the Gunpowder Pirates, and so the reception was even merrier than the first one.

"We should remarry every year!" Ruth proclaimed with delight.

The people laughed.

"Ruth and Roy truly love each other," Hannah said to Lily during the reception.

"They seem very happy," Lily said.

"Do you ever see yourself walking down the aisle?" Hannah asked.

"You will bite your tongue," Lily said. "To surrender my fortune to a man is unthinkable."

Hannah and Lily took a short journey to the southern coast of Devonshire and stared across the sea.

"To make a fortune on land only to have it taken away by sea-faring men," Lily said. "Again my attention is drawn to the sea and its ships. Mark my words, Hannah, something must be done about it."

Damien, as it turned out, was so furious at the news of losing the prospect of Ruth as a wife that he would have had Peter executed, had Peter survived the siege. Yes, Damien learned of the siege and made plans to find out more about this Hardshore family and its tentacles in business, but he disappeared suddenly without word of where or why, and so his pursuit of the matter seemingly ended. He had no children of his own to continue his pursuit, but he did have a brother and a nephew. It was they who took over his estate and studied his newly discovered records. The nephew in particular would watch and track the Hardshore family for some time, awaiting, awaiting, awaiting.

Chapter 19:

Alliance with the Consortium

The accomplishments of L M Hardshore Associates did not go unnoticed, especially by the competition. They were determined to thwart the Hardshore success in any way possible. They did this for raw materials, and in alternative fabrics.

Raw materials were not much of a problem for Lily, as Hannah helped establish connections for such. There were a couple of things, though, that Lily found too expensive. Tea for one. Lily lifted morale in her factories by providing for afternoon tea breaks. This not only allowed workers a bit of rest and social refreshment but also allowed them to voice concerns over production problems. Lily had managers take note of these concerns and factor them into process improvements. But tea was expensive, and so Lily needed to find a direct provider from the Far East.

Precious stones were another necessary commodity. The millwrights needed hard stones to make top-quality tools necessary to create and repair the machines needed for equally top-quality product.

But there was one other raw material that could change Lily's fortunes. Silk. Garments of silk and cashmere had been imported from India, and there was a growing interest in producing the same in England. One problem, however, was that silk could not be practically produced in Great Britain. The climate wasn't right. And so all silk had to be imported.

Another fabric industry that came to bear on Lily was cotton. But Lily wasn't fond of cotton. It was based on plants, something her father obsessed over, especially his heavy-cotton tarps that were unendingly moldy. Lily could never remove that scent of mold from her mind when "cotton" was mentioned, and so she avoided it.

Lily had produced a good cloth, but she wanted an excellent cloth. She had been following the maritime news long enough to know that it was time to see about the shipping business.

L M Hardshore Associates had worked with local shipping within Great Britain, of course. It was through those shippers (and several billiard games by "Hank") that Lily learned of a Captain Kent who had twice made sea-fairing voyages to the Orient. She had a letter sent to Captain Kent inquiring about his cargo to and from the Orient. His reply was that she contact the shipping company and join the venture as he was shipping soon, and it would take a year to complete the voyage.

"One year," Lily pondered. "A full season of crops. Shearings. Many afternoons of tea."

A year seemed a long time to wait, but Lily was determined. She had a letter of investment sent to the shipping company for Captain Kent's journey. It was agreed.

In the meantime, Lily prepared for weaving silk. Hannah discovered several French silk weavers who had escaped to England during the French Revolution. These weavers remained somewhat in hiding for fear of being persecuted by the English or taken back as traitors by the French. Lily put them to work immediately in one of her factories.

Then it dawned on Lily. The silkworm could survive in France. Silk could be produced much closer than the Orient. That's why there were French silk weavers. They had their own local supply. But France was still in turmoil. How could the country be tamed? It was beyond business sense, at least for the moment.

There was something else Lily learned from the French weavers. A company known as the DeBlanche Consortium was producing equipment for weaving—powered by steam.

Lily recognized the name "DeBlanche". It was that of her mother, as told to her by Carmichael. Her family in France had perished. But again, hopes of working with France were out of the question.

Expressing her discontent, the French weavers were quick to point out that the consortium was based in Ireland, that in fact the consortium also produced equipment to aid in mining.

Lily returned to the stable billiard room with Hannah to discuss. She told Hannah all about what she had just learned.

"Mining! Ireland!" Lily said.

"Of course," Hannah said. "Matter of fact, one of your copper mines is in Ireland."

"I...just remembered that," Lily said. "I'm afraid I have too many things to remember."

"I would not worry. Mr. Carmichael keeps track of everything, of course," Hannah said.

"Still, DeBlanche Consortium in Ireland," Lily said. "Could be a distant relative."

"Perhaps they migrated before the Revolution," Hannah said.

"Perhaps," Lily said.

Lily paced about the billiard table and looked upward as if in thought.

"You have an idea," Hannah grinned. "I can tell."

"What if?" Lily pondered aloud. "Fast transport to the Orient by steam. No doldrums. No yielding to the mercy of the sea. Direct and guaranteed."

"The Consortium?" Hannah added.

"Why not?" Lily said. "I have great experience with machines in our own factories, including steam engines. But to make them work for ships, that would be a new venture for me."

Lily and Hannah took the idea to Mr. Carmichael. He in turn drew up an introductory letter for a joint-venture between L M Hardshore Associates and DeBlanche Consortium.

With Ireland being just across the sea, it wasn't long before a reply was received. If agreed to, a chief designer would arrive to discuss this joint venture. Lily had Carmichael reply in agreement.

The chief designer, Sean, arrived at the Hardshore estate. Hannah attended as "Hank", Carmichael attended, and Lily attended too—posing as clerical help. "Hank" and Lily had a subtle form of sign language in use from many years of many prior meetings, and so "Hank" appeared to take the lead in technical matters.

The two sides respected each other for their technical knowledge and business savvy, and so they came to several agreements:

First, the two sides would collaborate on superior steam engine technology.

Second, DeBlanche Consortium would stay out of using steam engines for shipping in exchange for Roy sharing his rock blasting techniques for mining. Both companies would then collaborate on using steam drills for driving bore holes.

Third, DeBlanche Consortium would build the first superior steam engine using pistons and deliver it to L M Hardshore Associates for use in ship power. On its acceptance, an identical model would be built for DeBlanche's overseas mining operation in an undisclosed location, even secret from L M Hardshore Associates.

Fourth, DeBlanche would build a second but more powerful superior steam engine for use in its overseas mining. It would be more compact than the prior model, using a theoretical design called the "vane vortex" which was not yet proven.

Fifth, given the vane vortex engine be a success, DeBlanche would build that engine for L M Hardshore Associates for an even quicker ship.

Agreements were to be added or amended per future meetings.

Per the agreement, Roy and Ruth moved to Ireland to help the DeBlanche Consortium with mining techniques in steam drilling and blasting. Sean worked with them actively, keeping their work in a building separate from the main DeBlanche office (in order to protect secrets from both sides).

While Roy pioneered new blasting formulations, Ruth took to organizing and documenting the bore-hole testing efforts. This included determining the best drill bits, steam drills, and hole-placement techniques for quickly drilling the desired hole while controlling precisely how any give rockface would be sliced off. In order to help learn such techniques, she had to find a way to examine in detail the results of blast patterns to evaluate the effectiveness of Roy's gunpowder formulation.

For this effort, she enlisted the help of Gloria Frankenmuth. Gloria made a special trip to Ireland and started her own laboratory for the study of rock fragments. In this lab, Gloria had specially trained bees. Gloria set a blast-rock fragment in the middle of a suspended weave of very thin rush that the bees had woven. The weave was large, perhaps the size of a wide bed while the rock fragment itself was no larger than a penny. Atop the weave was placed a thin membrane with a fine layer of sand. The bees were then commanded to stand on the perimeter edge of the membrane and vibrate. As they did, they caused the sand to move slightly in resonance with the rush weave. In a sense, the ultra-fine crack pattern of the rock fragment, a pattern too small for the naked eye to see, was "magnified" and "projected" onto the sandy membrane, but instead of light being used for the projection, it was the bees' vibration on the rush weave that caused it.

At first, Ruth attempted to hand-draw what she saw on the sandy membrane. But this was a time consuming process, and often her drawings were not as well to scale or as realistic as the pattern portrayed on the membrane. She asked Gloria's advice on this. Gloria pondered the matter.

"There have been efforts to capture images quickly using lenses," Gloria said. "A dark chamber known as a *camera obscura* can render an image on a flat surface. But the flat surface does not retain the image. One must trace upon that surface to preserve the image. So far nothing has been able to preserve that image automatically. I have tried with my bees with various sorts of beeswax, but none capture the image."

An impasse of sorts came with Roy's blasting powder formulation. No matter what mixture he tried, it struggled to break apart hard rock. Test after test followed by Ruth's and Gloria's examination on the weave-membrane apparatus showed the same results—a lack of sufficient cracking necessary to shear off a slice of rock as needed.

Ruth and Gloria even took the risky approach of bringing samples of Roy's blasting powder to Gloria's lab so as to detonate small amounts on a bit of rock while it was on the rush weave, in hopes of seeing the problem. The first few efforts damaged the weave, but after having the bees strengthen the weave, the resulting pattern on the sandy membrane merely showed a broad yet gentle circular wave emanating from the center where the sample had been micro-blasted.

On one particular day while Ruth was collecting yet another blasting formulation from Roy, she became frustrated and threw the container across the room.

"This will not work," she said. "Day by day I take a sample for testing, and day by day the results are the same. The hardest of rocks cannot be blasted. This effort has become an unyielding obsession trapped in a ditch with no ladder out."

Roy was surprised to hear Ruth speak like this. She was right, of course. Seeing how the work effort was coming between their love, he immediately suggested they take leave of the work and rest at a secluded inn.

The two enjoyed a wonderful meal at the inn and took a leisurely walk along a path amongst the beautiful landscape. The sun chased a cloud toward the horizon, and the two found their love rekindled in the forest, where they shared this love amongst the carefree of the peaceful wild.

The light of the day faded before their passion, leading to dusk and darkness, and soon they saw a distant light, which they both took to be that from the inn. They headed back toward the light, but the ground seemed different and unsteady, as if they'd lost the path. In fact, they had.

"This doesn't feel right," Ruth said.

"The light is just ahead," Roy said. "We must follow it."

"But the path was smooth before," Ruth replied. "This ground is unsteady and yielding."

"I lost myself in your charm after having missed you for these many long days of work," Roy said. "I wanted to savor our love."

"We might lose it if we lose our way. Ugh. What is that smell? Oh!" Ruth said as her foot became stuck.

"It's a bog," Roy said.

"The light. It's a fool's light!" she said.

"You are right. Deceived by a Will O' the Wisp," Roy said. "Oft the traveler is beguiled by these lights."

"And led astray to their death! And ours!" Ruth said.

"King James will help us," Roy said.

Roy produced a hand-held flare and attempted to light it. But sparks from his tinder box lit nearby methane gas, causing the gas to ignite across the breadth of the bog. The sudden puff of flame lifted the two from their feet. Ruth and Roy didn't have time to yell, as they just as quickly landed in a large puddle on the edge of the bog, with mud as a companion.

Fortunately for them, they were only wet and not trapped in the mud, and so they lifted themselves to their feet and looked around.

"The Will O' the Wisp is gone," Roy said.

"You stink," Ruth said.

"We both do," Roy said. "This bog is filled with rotting muck. And yet somehow, I still have my tinderbox."

"Miracle of miracles, I have the flare. But it is wet," Ruth said.

"The flare is special and does not need to be dry. Here, hold it for me," Roy said.

Ruth shivered as Roy set to create a spark from his tinderbox.

"Do not be afraid," Roy said. "We should be safe from another blast of flame, at least for the moment."

Roy held Ruth's hand to reassure her. She regained her composure and then held the flare for him to light, which he did.

"I can see," Ruth said.

"Yes," Roy said. "Hold it above your head."

There was no sudden puff of great bog flame as before, but every so often, a puffball of flame about the size of an apple was ignited by the flare. It startled Ruth the first time, and she dropped the flare into a puddle at her feet, but the flare continued to burn underwater, and so it was easy to find and retrieve. Ruth reached to pick it up, but a bubble from the bog formed next to it, ignited, and puffed into flame by her hand. She jumped back in surprise.

Roy took the flare and lifted it above his head, despite other bubbles floating around and igniting. After a time, the two realized that they could smell these bubbles in the air as they approached, and so it became more of a game of keep away if the bubble chased them, or tag if they decided to chase these bubbles. In fact, Roy produced another flare, lit it from the first, and handed it to Ruth. The two then waved and slashed through the air to ignite these rogue bubbles of inflammable gas, and as these bubbles lit, they yelled at them to disperse and fade away, as if dispelling evil spirits away.

"Begone evil spirits of the bog," Ruth would say.

"Waylay travelers no more," Roy would say.

The two were able to find the path and return toward the inn. But just before they left the edge of the bog, they threw their flares in, so that the flares would prevent any "evil" spirits from following them to the inn. Meanwhile, there were refreshing spirits to consume inside the inn, to which they partook and celebrated their relief in refinding their way back to the inn, with cozy intimacy by a warm fire and clean furnishings. Fresh food was available, but romance of the evening precluded its need.

The next day, Roy and Ruth prepared to return from their holiday, but before they left the inn and its vicinity, they made for the bog where they'd thrown the flares. To their amazement, the flares had not been fully consumed but instead had fused with the nearby organic muck. Curious, Roy took the two pieces and placed them in his pack.

Roy and Ruth returned to Roy's gunpowder office, handed the fused flares to Sean, and walked outside the office to bid Ruth farewell.

"Wait for me at Gloria's lab," Roy said to her as he helped her into a carriage. "I'd like to learn more about this—"

But Roy was interrupted with a powerful explosion destroying a corner of his office. The carriage bolted off from fright with Ruth holding onto her seat and Roy clinging onto the outside. He managed to pull himself aside Ruth just as the driver settled the horse enough to slow, turn around, and return to the gunpowder office. People ran around in confusion, but it was Sean who ran up to Roy and Ruth to bring clarity to the deed.

"One of the pieces was placed under a crusher to crack it open," Sean said, covered in dirt. "It exploded. Some are hurt, but no one has died."

Roy and Ruth exchanged sighs of relief.

"I think you discovered something quite powerful," Sean said. "Powerful enough—"

"To blast through hard rock," Roy finished.

Roy had a lab set up by the bog. From there it wasn't long before Roy had a well-balanced formulation for blasting through the toughest of rock. Ruth was only able to test one sample, as it blasted the entire weave and encrusted the membrane sand against the ceiling. With the testing perfected, Ruth thanked Gloria for her help, allowing Gloria to return to her school for girls.

"Be sure to send any lost girls my way," Gloria said.

"Do not worry. No Will O' the Wisp will deceive them if I can help it," Ruth smiled, and Gloria left Ireland.

In the months that followed, DeBlanche Consortium was able to mine new veins previously unreachable by the old gunpowder formula. They never made known where these veins were, but a rumor made its way to L M Hardshore Associates that these new veins were a great help in developing steam engine technology. The vane vortex engine, once a whim of fantasy, was now within the realm of possibility.

Chapter 20:

The Shipping Business

A year had passed since the first agreements were made between L M Hardshore Associates and Captain Kent. Captain Kent did not arrive on time.

Lily became impatient. She hastened her work on an ocean steam ship, finding clever ways to conserve fresh water so as to minimize dealing with salt water for replenishment. She built a large enough steamship for cargo using the DeBlanche superior piston engine and ran it between port towns in Great Britain. This steam ship had working sails to blend in with other sail boats and thus not draw attention. Lily even managed to make a run over to Ireland and back. On its return, Lily had her machinists improve the steam engine design to minimize corrosion from salt water.

It had now been two years since Captain Kent had left for the Orient when word of his arrival reached the Hardshore estate. Lily was 25 years old by now (yes, the years seemed to fly by), and she was quite disappointed with his delay.

Lily was all but ready to launch her own steam ship (the Confidence) to the Orient when another bit of news had reached her. Actually, the "news" was a request for help from the DeBlanche Consortium. A cargo ship heading to the overseas mining site from Ireland had been chased and attacked in the Bay of Biscay. The ship crashed on Ushant, a French island at the south-western edge of the English Channel and just west of Brittany. The crew was hiding its cargo. This cargo was the first working prototype of the vane vortex engine.

Lily's heart dropped. The vane vortex engine. It could revolutionize power everywhere. But this was the summer of 1814, and France was still reeling from Napoleon, who had just fled to Elba in April of that year. If French forces found that engine, it would reinvigorate their effort, leading to a possible invasion of Britain and elsewhere.

The vane vortex engine had to be found and brought back to Ireland. But who could she trust? All interactions with shipping companies had been by letter from L M Hardshore Associates, but this was different. Lily needed to learn more about the regional captains without them suspecting her intent.

And so, one by one, Lily and "Hank" visited shipping companies and their captains. Lily always played the clerical person with the questions and documents to deliver, while "Hank" played the primary negotiator for standard shipping discussions. The topic of Ushant was not brought up directly, but Lily would drift amongst the crew and casually ask how was business with France and French islands, and so on.

After a long day of this (which meant traveling around quite a bit and at speed in the curricle), Lily and Hannah returned to the Hardshore estate, exhausted. One underlying theme came out of all regional captains and crews involved—no one was sailing to France or any French territories. The French Navy and people were hungry and desperate to the point of doing anything to any ship crossing their way.

The next day, Lily was resigned to using her own ship, the Confidence, to effect rescue. She would have to find a trustworthy crew willing to make the trip. Further, she would risk having her one and only steam ship captured. With Lily fretting and flailing at the fraughtful fate, Hannah reminded her that there was one captain in port who had yet to be interviewed.

"Captain Kent," Hannah said. "He isn't a regional captain, but he might be willing to try."

"And show up two years later," Lily sighed.

"I've met him. A captain of good integrity and respectful to his crew," Hannah said. "The story of his delay has come out. He was beleaguered by bad weather, pirates, and the capture of two crew members by the French Navy that he recovered. Not a single man has died under his command."

Lily paused.

"I shall witness for myself the integrity of Captain Kent," Lily said.

Lily had a letter of introduction drawn up from L M Hardshore Associates supposedly written from Lily's father (but of course was worded by Lily). Per Lily's instructions, "Hank" took Lily out to port with the curricle where Captain Kent's ship was docked.

"I'm going alone," Lily said.

"But your reputation," Hannah said.

"I have no reputation to worry about, as I have no reputation at all," Lily said. "If you want to help, though, spend time at the pub and learn what you can about Captain Kent."

Hannah agreed. She left the horses with a caretaker and spent time in a pub as "Hank" with beer, billiards, and buddies.

Chapter 21:

Dinner with Captain Kent

Lily walked up to "Pearl of the Sea", the registered ship name used by Captain Kent. It was a brigantine ship, but it was headed out to sea before she could reach it.

"He had not registered to leave," Lily unexpectedly said aloud, feeling disappointed to have missed Captain Kent.

"Begging your pardon, but who would that be?" asked a nearby sailor.

"Captain Kent," Lily said.

The sailor laughed.

"He is just leasing his old ship to a friend, Captain Allen. Captain Kent has a new ship now," the sailor said. "See?"

The sailor pointed to a Baltimore clipper ship with the name, "Lady Jack Nine".

"I have a letter of introduction for him from L M Hardshore Associates," Lily said. "If you would take me to him, please."

"Who should I say is calling?" the sailor asked.

"Miss Hardshore, daughter of Lord M Hardshore," Lily said.

The sailor agreed and took Lily aboard Lady Jack Nine. Lily was impressed at how clean and tidy the ship was. It smelled new, and even now there were crewmembers cleaning off leftover sawdust. The sailor introduced her. Captain Kent stood upon her arrival.

"Captain Kent, may I present Miss Hardshore, daughter of Lord M Hardshore," the sailor said. "She has a letter of introduction from L M Hardshore Associates."

The sailor left as Lily and Captain Kent exchanged looks. Both were stunned. Captain Kent did not realize Lord M had such a beautiful daughter, and Lily did not realize Captain Kent was so strikingly handsome. After several seconds, Lily handed the letter to Captain Kent.

His eyes had difficulty pulling away from Lily's charm. Both could only smile and smile. Finally, he read the note aloud, particularly the part about giving all courtesy to Lily as his daughter and treat her as his proxy since he no longer travels.

"Is this a warship?" Lily asked in a soft feminine voice.

Captain Kent laughed.

"It could be with some imagination," he joked.

"You would win every battle. Bring peace to the world," Lily flirted.

"Permit me to show you around," Captain Kent said, and he did.

As he showed her around, she had a few questions about how cargo was sold and the money divided. Just curious. Captain Kent was enchanted with her keen mind yet soft demeanor, and so he invited her to dinner. She accepted.

Dinner was in a fine establishment within visual observation of the pub, where "Hank" was able to continue her covert information gathering while watching her keep.

As it turned out, there were few words spoken. Instead, an exchange of body language took place between Captain Kent and Lily.

After the two had a bite to eat, Lily managed to convince Captain Kent to explain his part in the trade system. Lily wanted to learn all she could about the trade business, but she was especially interested in Captain Kent himself. She learned that he grew up in Ireland but often visited England. A tall and handsome man, Captain Kent had dark red hair and chiseled features.

"I would like to see you again," Captain Kent said at the end of dinner. "May I call on you?"

Lily giggled in response, saying, "Yes."

The two had nearly parted ways, when instead she glanced out the window toward the pub and caught a glimpse of "Hank" reminding her of her original purpose.

"There is something, my charming man of good wisdom. A package for pickup. A package for..."

Lily's voice trailed, as words failed her from the gaze of Captain Kent's enamor. Instead, she produced a letter and handed it to him.

"'L M Hardshore Associates seek reliable captain to transport special cargo to Ireland,'" Captain Kent read aloud. "It does not say where the cargo is."

"You shan't," Lily said, gazing dreamily in his eyes.

"I shan't what?" he replied.

"Oh," she said. "I mispronounced it."

"It?"

"An island. At the edge of the English Channel," she said.

"The English Channel," Captain Kent mused. "Must be a special cargo for such a short journey. Hardly any time at all compared to the Orient."

"It's the island of Ushant," Lily said.

Lily produced another document and handed it to the captain.

"The Fenscott, a cargo ship for the DeBlanche Consortium, left Ireland on the way to...this part is smudged out," Captain Kent said. "Ship was chased, attacked, and crashed on Ushant. Cargo can be identified by these three wine leaves etched on the container of five lobes, three, and three. Captain Mortimer and crew are prisoners. Interesting. The rescue is for the cargo, not the captain and crew."

"It is a business," Lily started to say, but her voice softened as she felt her affection for Captain Kent continue to grow, "but people must be safe. You must be safe. Will you go? I was thinking of going. Oh, I'm rambling so."

"It is unsafe for you to go," Captain Kent said. "Nor would I wish to place you in harm's way. I will leave first thing in the morning."

"I wish...wish to see you off," Lily said.

The two arranged to meet by the Lady Jack Nine in the morning. Lily signaled to "Hank", and "he" came round with the curricle to pick up Lily.

"Until tomorrow," Captain Kent said as he disappeared into the night.

"Oh, I cannot think," Lily said to "Hank".

"I believe you have an affection for him," said "Hank". "This for the man who is a year late."

"I will never know the year that was lost," Lily dreamed.

"Should we visit his ship? Right now?" said "Hank". "Take a moonlight stroll."

"Oh no, I feel that I would lose myself," Lily said. "Everything is happening too quickly. I must re-find myself. I...my steamboat. The Confidence. Take me there."

The Confidence was not far away. Lily and "Hank" arrived there shortly, and the two boarded. A skeleton crew manned the ship and casually greeted the two.

"My ship seems different somehow. So flat and barren," Lily said. "It needs color. Lots of colorful paint with floral patterns divine."

"The ship is the same," said "Hank". "It is you who have changed."

"I should invite him aboard. We could dance the night away," Lily said.

"That you should *not* do," said "Hank". "This is still a man's world. You might lose favor with him, should he see the marvel you have created."

Lily danced around the ship by herself. A crewmember motioned for "Hank" as if wishing to show "him" something. "Hank" ventured over, took a look at a flashing light over the water, and then blacked out.

Chapter 22:

Kidnapped

Hannah came to. Yes, Hannah. Her disguise had fallen off or otherwise. She found herself pulling herself to shore at port, not far from where the Confidence was docked. It was dawn, and she could see a nearby crewmember, Jacques, who had also pulled himself to shore sitting there and smoking to relieve his shaking. Rubbing the backside of her head where she had apparently received a blow, she limped over to him.

"What happened to you?" she asked.

"The Confidence. It was stolen. With Miss Lily aboard," Jacques said. "I was thrown over. Who are you?"

Hannah looked around and yes, the Confidence was no longer in port. She gave out a loud whistle as loud as she could, a whistle meant for the horses. Climbing a bank to a road with Jacques, she could hear the faint gallop of her two horses. Well trained and well poised, they halted upon reaching Hannah, with the curricle still attached.

With great speed, she and Jacques took the curricle back to the Lady Jack Nine. It was still in port. Desperate, she rushed up to the ship and asked for Captain Kent. Captain Kent showed up, but he did not recognize Hannah. She quickly explained that she was a friend of Lily's, was on a new ship of Lily's, the Confidence, and it was apparently stolen, with Lily aboard.

When Captain Kent heard that Lily was aboard, his pallor drained, and he let out a light gruff as if struggling to hold himself up from a sudden weight pressing down on his heart.

"I saw the way they went," the crewmember said. "Created their own cloud into the dawn sky."

Captain Kent seemed puzzled by the description of a ship creating a cloud, but it was no matter. The crewmember clearly saw where the Confidence went, and that was good enough for him. He ordered the Lady Jack Nine crew to prepare for launch, inviting the Confidence crewmember along as a guide. Hannah requested to go as well. Captain Kent declined, but she insisted that she had specific knowledge about the Confidence, about Lily, and about the package in Ushant.

"I must forego the package. Lily comes first," Captain Kent said. "But you must notify her family, Hannah. Lord M must know."

Hannah quickly wrote up a letter and arranged for its delivery to Lord M, advising of the situation. Again she demanded to go, and again Captain Kent would not allow it, finally saying that he could not jeopardize her safety as well. He promised to bring Lily back to safety.

Lady Jack Nine departed. It took on great speed, as the winds were favorable. Weather held up, visibility was excellent, and soon Jacques helped Captain Kent find small puffs of clouds on the distant horizon.

"There is some devilry about that ship," Captain Kent said. "A sailboat that creates clouds."

"It is not meant to create clouds," Jacques said.

Captain Kent then pressed Jacques about the Confidence. Jacques explained that yes, it had sails, but it also had a mechanical device that helped propel the ship along, using a coal furnace to heat water into the steam. The steam drove an engine, yes, but the steam was then cooled and reused, as the ocean's salt water was too corrosive to use exclusively.

"A steam boat," Captain Kent said. "I have heard of them. It must be incredibly advanced to hold such speed ahead of the Lady Jack Nine."

Captain Kent then asked who could have stolen the Confidence. Jacques, being fluent in English and French, admitted that he heard French shouting when the Confidence was stolen. Jacques was convinced therefore that whoever it was, was French.

"First there is the Fenscott being attacked by the French. Now the Confidence is stolen," Captain Kent said. "Both ships are related to L M Hardshore Associates. Are the actions also related?"

Lady Jack Nine caught an exceptional wind, and it gained quickly on the Confidence, almost too quickly. Several shots were fired from the Confidence toward Lady Jack Nine.

"You said nothing about weapons on the Confidence," Captain Kent said to Jacques.

"It had none. The capturer must have brought them aboard," Jacques said.

The Lady Jack Nine crew asked if they should fire back.

"You have weapons too?" Jacques said.

"We *are* at war with France. Must take precautions," Captain Kent said.

Captain Kent gave the order for but one round of fire, then to stop, as he was fearful that he might kill Lily in the process. The Confidence stopped firing and in fact stopped voluntary movement, merely drifting along with the current.

"Approach it cautiously. Not too close," Captain Kent said. "Could be a trick."

Without warning, the Confidence vented a great plume of steam. But instead of rising up immediately, it enshrouded the ship. Faint voices and light splashing could be heard momentarily from the steam, but it quickly abated. The steam cleared, and the Confidence was still there, though its sails had been withdrawn.

"Now for it," Captain Kent called.

Captain Kent ordered the Lady Jack Nine to intercept the Confidence with weapons at the ready. He expected gunfire in return, and his crew was prepared for a fight. Strangely, however, there was no fight. The Lady Jack Nine came alongside the Confidence, and Captain Kent led the way across to the Confidence, with guns and swords at the ready.

They found no crew. Captain Kent searched frantically, but no one was aboard. Then, in a lower hold, he heard a muffled sound. Jacques helped Captain Kent open a hatch where they found Lily bound, blindfolded, and gagged.

"You're safe!" Captain Kent said.

Lily tried to speak, but she could only shake in exhaustion. Captain Kent picked her up, and she immediately fell into shock.

Captain Kent's crew made way for the captain to bring Lily aboard Lady Jack Nine, but Jacques pointed out the danger considering the seas, the unsteady relation between the two ships, and Lily's condition. Captain Kent agreed, and so Lily would stay aboard the Confidence for a little while. Knowing the layout of the ship, Jacques led the captain and Lily to special quarters, where Captain Kent made her comfortable.

As Jacques tended to the Confidence, Captain Kent tended to Lily. He gave her food and drink, and then worked to restore circulation in her arms and feet, as the restraints had been terribly tight.

"Can you hear me?" Captain Kent said with deep concern.

"Uh...I...who is it?" Lily said in a daze.

Captain Kent held her hand. She weakly squeezed back with a faint sense of growing trust.

"It's Captain Kent," he said. "Captain Killian Kent."

"Your name," she said with growing strength. "Killian. Such strength for a gentle man."

"It is only for you to say," he said. "I am still Captain Kent to the world."

As Lily improved, she told the story of her kidnapping. A Frenchman named Andre DeVille snuck onto her ship and overpowered her crew quietly. Hannah was with her at the time, but to where Hannah went, Lily did not know.

"Hannah found me and told me she received a blow to the head. She is safe at port," Captain Kent said.

Lily smiled, and her pallor improved. Andre had tracked her down because she was involved with the DeBlanche Consortium, and Andre was pursuing the

DeBlanche family fortune. Andre suspected Lily was herself of the DeBlanche family.

"I do not understand," Captain Kent said. "Begging your pardon, but Lord M was married to Colleen of Dalbarth. Of Scotland."

Lily paused.

"I am not a Dalbarth," Lily finally mustered, afraid to admit that her true parents were never married. "My father is a Hardshore, and my mother is a DeBlanche. I left France for England when I was four."

Captain Kent paused, then he suddenly laughed.

"Do you think this amusing?" she said, with a bit of fire catching her tongue.

"No, not at all," he said, settling down. "I was afraid you were half Scottish. I was truly afeard."

Now Lily laughed.

"Before you pass on to a fit of elegance, my father is Irish and my mother English," he said. "You know how the Irish feel about the Scottish."

"Or how the English feel about the French," Lily said.

"So if I lean to the Irish, I be afeard of the Dalbarth Scottish, and if I lean to the English, I be afeard of the French DeBlanche," Captain Kent said. "From which side shall my blood divide?"

"I am Lily Hardshore. English," she said. "Let English enjoy the company of English. I have some tea on board somewhere."

Captain Kent laughed.

"Now I know you are English," he continued to laugh. "Here we are on the high seas, fresh from danger and torture, and yet tea becomes priority one."

Lily made to get up, but she slumped back.

"I could use a cup of tea. With you. Please?" she asked.

Captain Kent called for Jacques, and he had tea drawn from stores, prepared, and served.

"Andre intends to marry me to acquire the DeBlanche family fortune," Lily said quietly. "He thinks I know where it is."

"Do you?" Captain Kent asked.

Lily remained motionless.

"My apologies. I should not ask," he said.

"He thinks a DeBlanche family fortune is in France," she said. "He was using me to find it, after which I would no longer remain pure."

"You are safe with me," Captain Kent reassured her.

But at that moment, the echoes of cannon fire were followed by a cannon ball landing in the water nearby. Captain Kent went out to look. He saw a distant frigate ship firing on them. Lady Jack Nine immediately separated and took to maneuvers while Captain Kent ordered Jacques to assist in getting the Confidence into maneuvers. Adjusting the rigs was slow work, as there weren't enough people to help. Captain Kent himself went down below to assist Jacques in getting the steam engine going, but when he did, Jacques opened a secret hatch, allowing hidden French men to flood the area.

Surprised by this betrayal, Captain Kent had no chance and was immediately captured. He was taken above deck where he watched the frigate come closer. It became apparent that this was a French frigate. Special puffs of steam rose from the Confidence, and even Captain Kent could tell that these were friendly signals sent to the frigate. Lady Jack Nine, having only simple guns, could only take brief runs at the frigate, fire, then sail back away.

A lucky shot from the frigate caught Lady Jack Nine, and she lost most of her sails. She had only enough wind to barely navigate, but not enough to get away. In comparison to the frigate and the Confidence, she was adrift.

The frigate reached the Confidence, and Captain Kent saw its name, "Tragus".

"An ugly name for an ugly ship," Captain Kent muttered.

But his words were heard, and he suffered a blow to the head. Stunned but alert, he watched as the captain of the Tragus motioned toward a tall, burly man with a heavy scar on his left face, scraggly beard, and broken teeth.

"I present Andre DeVille," the captain said.

Loyal crew acknowledged Andre as a courtesy. Captain Kent did not, and so Andre, after boarding the Confidence, stared Captain Kent gruffly in the eyes. Andre's foul breath was worse than any dead animal he had encountered, and it was all Captain Kent could do to remain conscious during the effort.

"This is Captain Kent," Jacques said, now on board. "He and his crew followed you in Lady Jack Nine."

Jacques pointed to first Captain Kent and then Lady Jack Nine as he spoke.

"So you be pirates? Privateers?" Andre said.

"The Confidence does not belong to you. It is owned by L M Hardshore Associates," Captain Kent said. "I am effecting its return."

Andre and the others laughed.

"Under what flag?" Andre said. "You are in French waters. You have no say here."

"Nevertheless, your act constitutes—"

"War," Andre said. "But we are already at war with the British. And since you take their part, you forfeit any French right, which I claim over this ship and its contents."

"I am a captain. With my own ship," Captain Kent said.

"A man with no ship is no captain," Andre said.

At that moment, an incendiary shot was fired at Lady Jack Nine. It caught fire with its sails going up in great flame.

"No more Lady Jack Nine," Andre said. "And no more captain."

With that, Captain Kent was shoved overboard. He treaded water to stay afloat and attempted to find a way aboard the Confidence, but without much luck. A crewmember loyal to the French brought Lily to the deck for Andre to gawk over.

"What kind of man abandons the Confidence only to regain it?" Captain Kent shouted as the Confidence began pulling away.

"You have answered your own question," Andre shouted back.

The frigate also began pulling away. The last Captain Kent heard across the water was a shout from Andre.

"See if you can regain yours."

Chapter 23:

The Island of Ushant

Captain Kent, with Lily disappearing into the distance one way and his Lady Jack Nine in tatters in the other, felt despair. But he did not give up. Using floating debris to conserve energy, he swam toward Lady Jack Nine. Lady Jack Nine in turn ambled toward Captain Kent as best as possible, but the effort was slow, taking several hours.

At length, Captain Kent was pulled aboard what was left of Lady Jack Nine. All sails were burned, the masts broken beyond immediate repair, and the ship took on water that required constant bailing. Everywhere Captain Kent looked, he saw nothing but charred black wood. His crew had worked as hard as they could to put out the fire to save the craft, but the craft was weak and was vulnerable to breaking apart should a storm come their way.

Lady Jack Nine drifted for a day and night. The next day, another ship approached from the horizon. Was it friend or foe? Either way, there was nothing to do but wait.

As the ship approached, it became clear it was a brigantine, and an English ship at that. The crew cheered as they recognized their old ship, The Pearl of the Sea. Captain Kent was taken aboard by Captain

Allen as soon as the ships met. To his surprise, Hannah was there.

"I am pleased but puzzled at this meeting," Captain Kent said.

Captain Allen then explained how he returned to port shortly after going out to repair a leak.

"Here I thought you loaned me a good ship," Captain Allen smirked.

Captain Allen went on to explain how he bumped into Hannah, who convinced him to catch up with Lady Jack Nine to help with Lily's return. They were astounded to find Lady Jack Nine in such condition.

Captain Kent quickly told of his encounter with the Confidence, Lily, Andre, and the attack on Lady Jack Nine. He included Andre's desire to acquire the DeBlanche family fortune by marrying Lily, a fortune that Andre believed to be in France.

Captain Allen pointed out that he had heard of the DeVille name, and if this be the same Andre DeVille of stories told, Andre was the nephew of Damien DeVille, a man of ill repute and dirty deals, and so the family name "DeVille" should be taken with caution and concern. Further, Damien was unaccounted for of late and could be involved.

Crews worked together to get a bit of a sail working on Lady Jack Nine. Meanwhile, the two captains and Hannah discussed the next course of action. As it turned out, the two ships were closer to Ushant than any other landmass. Hannah mentioned the original mission to Ushant, to which Captain Kent was surprised. Lily's life was at stake here.

Hannah pulled Captain Kent aside.

"I am concerned about Lily too," Hannah said. "That's why I say we go to Ushant. It's not just the package. It's what the package contains. I hesitate to say in front of the others. In fact, I hesitate to say at all."

"Then do not. Spies are everywhere, it seems," Captain Kent said. "Betrayal is just one wayward crewmember nigh."

"One thing you can be sure of," Hannah said. "The package will help us, if we can retrieve it."

"The three grape leaves of five lobes, three, and three," Captain Kent said.

"Yes," Hannah said. "But it isn't wine or anything for consumption. I will say no more, except that we should make for Ushant and the package immediately."

Captain Kent was unsure.

"Lily," Captain Kent pondered. "I would sail the entire Bay of Biscay for her."

"And never find her," Hannah said. "But I know Lily. First, she will try to divert this Andre away from mainland France, especially where the DeBlanche family is from—the Loire Valley. Anything to gain time."

"Reasonable," Captain Kent said.

"The best way for her to do so without being so obvious is to make up a wild story," Hannah said.

"And that would be?"

"A diamond mine," Hannah said.

Captain Kent laughed.

"I know something of trade, Hannah," Captain Kent said with authority. "India is the place for precious stones, especially diamonds. Quite a sailing distance from France."

"But tell me, Captain Kent," Hannah continued. "If such a diamond mine could be conquered closer by, would it not be quicker for trade? For building wealth and power?"

For a moment, Captain Kent felt a surge of energy, as if there *were* a diamond mine close-by.

"L M Hardshore Associates has been successful in mining of its own," Hannah explained. "Lily could use that knowledge to make a convincing case. I'm almost sure of it."

"Such a petite and charming girl," Captain Kent started.

"Could be as petite and charming to Andre as a way to buy us time to find her," Hannah said. "But the Confidence is a fast ship."

"Until Lady Jack Nine caught it," Captain Kent said. "But that was a trap. To satisfy his ego."

Captain Kent made a fist and slammed it against a beam.

"What is in that package? What?" he pressed.

"A way to catch the Confidence," Hannah returned.

Captain Kent smiled. Then smiled again.

"Yes, we shall go, but under a different flag," he said.

Hannah was puzzled.

"You have your secret, and I have mine," he returned.

Hannah smiled.

The two captains got together and made plans. "Pearl of the Sea" became "Pearl of Fortune", a bounty ship with no allegiance to any country. Hannah and Captain Allen stayed aboard her while Captain Kent took command of Lady Jack Nine, which was "escorted" into Ushant as a "captive English ship".

It was convincing. The French at Ushant believed that Lady Jack Nine was being turned in for a reward. In fact, the "Pearl of Fortune" crew put up quite a convincing act at demanding their reward, but in the end, the French thanked the Pearl of Fortune before they were fired upon to be taken as a prize themselves.

Pearl of Fortune left, but not too far. It waited far enough from Ushant not to be seen but within easy sailing distance as needed.

Captain Kent and two crewmembers were aboard Lady Jack Nine but hidden. The French tugged Lady Jack Nine into a harbor within sight of the crashed Fenscott. The French joked about the "poor wisdom of the British Isles" while rummaging through Lady Jack Nine, mainly for food of all things (they were hungry).

Captain Kent, however, had only a smattering of things left out for the French to find. He had his main stores hidden, and he kicked himself for not searching the Confidence for hidden stores when he first rescued Lily. Had he done so and not let his senses sway him, he might have her in his arms now. Instead, he had the dirty boot of a crewmember in his arm.

One thing he left out in the open and not hidden was the supply of booze. The French raiders took liberties with such and soon found themselves inebriated as the day wore on. By night, the French had deserted Lady Jack Nine, for which Captain Kent and his crewmembers were thankful, as the stench from the spilled booze had permeated the porous wood (porous from being burned) and seeped into every one of its fibers.

A strange quiet came over the ship. Almost too quiet. Captain Kent and his crew snuck out and realized why. A storm was approaching from the west, with the heavy sound of waves preparing to crash in. The three searched for cover. Being difficult to see, they made for a lighthouse.

They never made it. An outpouring of rain caught them. The three tripped over plots in a cemetery, and they ended up taking refuge in a maintenance shed.

The storm was fierce, but the shed held, and the three managed to get a little rest late in the night as the storm abated. By early dawn, it was all over, and the three, though weary, snuck out.

Yes, they were still on cemetery grounds, but what surprised Captain Kent was that certain headstones had the carvings of three grape leaves—lobes of five, three, and three. Captain Kent realized it was a sign. The three pieced together the position of these headstones and realized it created an arrow, pointing to a freshly dug grave.

Captain Kent could barely contain his excitement. The package was buried in a grave. But then he realized the flaw in the plan, either from fatigue or proceeding too quickly. How was he to get it out? The Pearl of the Sea was out to sea, and Lady Jack Nine was lifeless when it docked and most likely fully wrecked by the storm.

As it turned out, he was being watched. Crewmembers of the Fenscott had been spying on the cemetery, awaiting the day someone would notice the signs, friend or foe, and make an appropriate response.

They did.

Turns out, they had been hiding in the very lighthouse that Captain Kent and his two men had headed for. The Fenscott crew gradually surrounded the three to make that friend-or-foe determination.

It did not take long to convince them. Captain Kent still had documents of their situation from L M Hardshore Associates.

The group took shelter in the lighthouse in a secret meeting. There Captain Kent shared his news with the Fenscott crew, and their news with him. It was there that Captain Kent learned the contents of the package, a new pistonless steam engine known as the "vane vortex" engine. It was meant for a mining colony, inland from the Cape of Good Hope at the southern part of Africa.

"The engine could power a ship," said one of the Fenscott crew.

The Fenscott crew contemplated fitting it to a ship to escape Ushant, but their own ship was beyond hope other than for spare parts, and there were no others they could commandeer without notice. They needed time to work. But they would change their plans to help Captain Kent. All agreed that Lily's rescue was most important.

Captain Kent, after being given a disguise by the Fenscott crew, took a casual walk to where Lady Jack Nine was supposed to be. But it wasn't. The storm had pulled it out to sea and then beached it, ironically closer to the lighthouse from where he'd just been. No one was around, and so he went to examine the ship.

The hull was covered with dead ocean life, in fact, it was a wonder Captain Kent recognized the ship at all. But the masts were still broken as he remembered, and so that's how he knew. He brushed away the dead ocean life from a particular part of the hull, and he realized that lightning must have hit the ship, causing a lower layer of ocean life to harden over like glazed pottery. He knocked on this spot, and though hard to the touch, it had a vacuous sound from within, suggesting it was nearly hollow.

Captain Kent pushed against the hull, and he was able to rock it just a slight little bit, impossible if the hull were made of its original material. But it budged. He rushed back to the lighthouse to let them know what he found, and they made immediate preparations to have Lady Jack Nine pulled to an inlet and to a farmer sympathetic to their cause, where the boat was hidden under cover.

The Fenscott crew dug up the vane vortex engine under cover of another funeral and transported it to the farmhouse. Why had they not done that before? They were afraid the farmer would be caught. They still were, but if they moved quickly, they could get the engine installed on the Lady Jack Nine and back out to sea before the farmer was caught.

With everyone working, they were able to do so. It wasn't easy, as the Fenscott crew was only used to installing engines for driving mining equipment and not ships, but they made it work. Under cover of night, Captain Kent, his two crewmembers, and the Fenscott crew all left Ushant on Lady Jack Nine.

Chapter 24:

Andre's Confidence

Lily. She was under the close eye of Andre DeVille on the Confidence and headed for the mouth of the Loire River, France. Andre had paid off the frigate captain for his services, who in turn sailed off in search of food for his crew.

"That Captain Kent is a fool, to be so easily lured into a trap," Andre said to Lily as the two sat for breakfast. "But there is a greater task at hand. You."

"I do not understand," Lily said to gain time.

"You are a DeBlanche, daughter of Lady Antoinette DeBlanche," Andre said. "This I know. I also know the DeBlanche family has a great fortune that was never found. You will be my bride, and I will have rights to that fortune—legally. It will only be a matter of time before it is found. I know you were in France until you were four. We will spend time together, refreshing your memory and the location of the fortune."

Andre recited part of the poem:

> *DeBlanche are so Franch*
> *From Valley are Loire*

Lily hid her surprise that Andre seemed to know the poem. Or did he? Had he known the rest, he might have figured out the location of the family fortune. Up to this point, Lily didn't realize there was a family fortune or why she was made to memorize the poem when she was four. But now she was 25, and things did fit together—the poem contained directions for retrieving a family fortune. She dare not tell him the rest, lest he have his way with her and take the fortune outright. She must remain pure.

"Where do we go, Lily? Where?" Andre pressed.

Lily held silent. Andre then bragged about his shrewd, savvy ability to organize men of the sea. He was particularly impressed with the Confidence being run by steam and bragged about how easily steam allowed him to manipulate the situation with Captain Kent. He bragged further that the steam technology in the Confidence would allow him to build a navy equal or even superior to the French Navy and launch a coup on France while it was still weak from Napoleon's exile to Elba.

But he needed more funding. And he pressured Lily. Would she rather see Napoleon return to France and cause terror again, causing grief not only to French people, but to British people as well who would be drawn into further unending years of war, possibly falling under control of Napoleon himself? She would be a nobody, locked away as a seamstress in a forgotten factory repairing soiled uniforms of dead soldiers so that other soldiers could die in the same cloth.

Or she could help him make swift end of the French-British conflict and bring peace to the region.

"I give you time to think about things," Andre said. "When we reach the mouth of the Loire River, I will have your allegiance, one way or another."

The Confidence continued onward south in the Bay of Biscay toward the mouth of the Loire River. Andre had such great confidence in his plan that he allowed Lily free roam of the ship, as if to say that she was a trusted member of the crew.

Lily's nerves were deeply frayed, so deeply that at times she felt reality and past memories mixing. The idea that Andre was using her and would then be rid of her was ever-present. Given Andre was close in age to her father (and again with her near delirium), she formed a half-split image in her mind of her father wanting to be rid of her for personal gain and this Andre character of the same. The divided contrasted comparison echoed deep dissonance in her spirit, and she found herself mingling with the crew as she had done with the servants of the Hardshore estate.

Any sane person would have done nothing to help, but Lily, out of a desperate reach for sanity, fell back on her design and mathematical skills for an escape. She explained various features of the ship to crewmembers, how they could avoid being hurt, and how to avoid frustration.

Lily made particular friends with Pierre, a slave who was captured from Africa when very young but who now spoke English and French. Lily mentioned how the water of the ocean is trapped in a mixture of salt, and only when it rises to the heavens into clouds can it shake free the binds of salt. Pierre particularly identified with this description, and the two made plans for something that would help them both.

It was this way then. The Confidence approached Saint-Nazaire, a fishing village at the mouth of the Loire River. Lily then "let slip" a recent document about her business with DeBlanche Consortium for a site near the Cape of Good Hope in southern Africa. Andre pressed her for what this was about, and she "admitted" that there was a diamond mine there. She didn't really know of course, but she had to do something to gain time, and as Hannah predicted to Captain Kent, this was what she thought of (besides, it worked with her plan with Pierre).

"A diamond mine. In Africa," he mused. "I have heard no such word."

"No one has," Lily said under duress.

"If you are lying," he threatened with a fist.

"L M Hardshore Associates needs the diamonds for machine tools," Lily said, which was true, but then she realized that maybe there *was* a diamond mine in Africa, and this was where DeBlanche Consortium was getting them so quickly and cheaply, but it also meant pulling DeBlanche Consortium into her predicament.

Could she expect help from them? Perhaps.

"So someone *does* know," Andre said. "Your Hardshore family business."

"They only pay for the diamonds, they don't know if it comes from my French family," Lily said.

It was true that L M Hardshore Associates didn't know from where the diamonds came, and DeBlanche Consortium of Ireland made the stipulation that their mining was in an undisclosed location, but Lily did surmise its location and of course had the letter ready in case she needed to use it (as she often did for business ventures).

Andre took anchor at Saint-Nazaire. He had already arranged for a shipment of coal to be loaded from there, and so Pierre went out on a longboat to arrange for the coal to be loaded, which it was.

Provisions for the long voyage were also brought out, enough for reaching the Cape and back. Given how well the Confidence performed in the Bay of Biscay, Andre looked forward to a speedy trip to the Africa diamond mine, a trip in which no other sailboat could compete.

Now Lily knew that Captain Kent, despite the situation in which she had last seen him, would come after her. But she felt it important to give him a clue as to where he could find her. This was Pierre's part.

Pierre had cleverly borrowed a longboat from shore that resembled the ones on the Confidence, and so as the Confidence began pulling away, it had all of its longboats aboard, plus one that no one noticed, because just as this extra longboat was nearly pulled up, Lily set fire in the boiler room, a fire that put out more black smoke than anything, but it provided enough cover and diversion such that Pierre could (and did) take the extra longboat back down to the sea and slip away to shore.

The charred remains of what appeared to be Pierre were found in the boiler room, remains that were actually of a dead animal secretly brought aboard earlier by Pierre and left with Lily for her to plant when the "fire" went off. Lily herself was found nowhere near the boiler room but instead "safe" in her quarters.

Andre ordered a count of the longboats, and yes, all were accounted for. So was the crew, except for Pierre.

And so, the conclusion was that he had died, when instead he had been liberated by the smoke of a steamboat.

Chapter 25:

Discovery at Saint-Nazaire

Captain Kent and Lady Jack Nine rendezvoused with "Pearl of Fortune", which had kept its shady appearance in case of French interception. Hannah boarded Lady Jack Nine to meet with Captain Kent. There, Hannah was shown the work done by the Fenscott crew with the vane vortex engine.

"I have only heard about it," Hannah said with amazement, "but to see it in action, a true marvel of the ages."

Though Lady Jack Nine was fast, she was low on food provisions, fresh water, and coal. Further, Captain Kent wasn't sure if Lily could convince Andre to avoid the Loire River or not. They would need to travel to Saint-Nazaire to make a determination. It might also be a chance to acquire needed supplies, though as Captain Kent pointed out, this was France. However, with Pearl of Fortune still looking as it did and Lady Jack Nine still looking charred and burned, Captain Kent felt the French would more or less laugh than desire to capture either.

They both went in, then, to Saint-Nazaire. Sailing up the Loire River was not a common thing, but a steam ship like the Confidence could have attempted it, and that was what worried Captain Kent. As he was looking for volunteers to make first contact with the locals, it was Hannah who stepped forward. Turned out she also knew French, having been taught basics from Lily back in the day and learned further from the French weavers back at one of the L M Hardshore Associates factories.

And so, Hannah disguised as "Hugo Ruse", played billiards, made bets, drank, and got to know the locals. She won these bets, many bets, and when locals couldn't pay, she arranged through clever means for the purchase of food, fresh water, and unbelievably—coal.

"Hugo" also met up with Pierre. Pierre had heard about Hannah from Lily, and so he made an impromptu drawing of three grape leaves with lobes of five, three, and three. "Hugo" realized that Pierre had important news, and he did. He told Hannah all about how he had been made a slave to serve Andre, track down Lily, capture the Confidence, trap Captain Kent, and how Lily convinced Andre that there was a diamond mine in Africa.

That confirmed it for Hannah. She immediately made Pierre an offer to come aboard and find Lily in return for his freedom as a British citizen. He agreed.

Although "Hugo" secured ownership of the provisions, it was Pierre who helped with its delivery to Saint-Nazaire and subsequent loading to Pearl of Fortune or Lady Jack Nine as appropriate. When all were ready to leave, "Hugo" removed "his" disguise and revealed her identity as Hannah to Pierre. Pierre was impressed.

Hannah had made another discovery while shooting billiards, and she relayed this discovery on meeting back with Captain Allen and Captain Kent.

"Damien DeVille is presumed dead," she said. "He left for Lower Canada and has not been heard from since. Some say his heart failed. Others say he was taken away by gentle angels while performing acts of kindness to fellow men."

"Acts of kindness to fellow men?" Captain Allen laughed. "Heart failure is the more likely."

"Nevertheless, his local terror in Europe has ended, at least by his hand," Hannah said. "Locals say his brother and nephew have taken over in his stead."

"His nephew. Andre DeVille," Captain Allen added.

"Yes," Hannah said.

"One discovery begets another," Captain Kent said. "I must make for the Cape with the greatest of speed."

It was this way then. Lady Jack Nine with Pierre helping in the boiler room and Captain Kent in command raced ahead southward toward the Cape of Good Hope. The Pearl of Fortune dropped her shady appearance and returned to being "Pearl of the Sea". She was no match in speed for Lady Jack Nine, but that was the agreement. She would continue toward the Cape of Good Hope with the idea she would arrive after Lily's rescue had been effected.

Or carry news of defeat back to England.

Hannah wasn't happy about being "left behind" yet again, but she made the best of things aboard Pearl of the Sea. Matter of fact, she took to Captain Allen, as well as he took to her. So in a sense, it was a bit fortuitous for her. They stood on the deck and looked outward to the sea.

"Do you remember when we first met?" Hannah asked.

"Yes," Captain Allen said. "In Ireland. One of my men had just been hustled in a game of billiards and wanted me to seek recompense against this scoundrel known as 'Hank'. I went to see who this scoundrel was, only to realize that 'Hank' was a woman in disguise. You had fooled everyone but me."

"I thought you would report me as a fraud," Hannah said. "Instead, you invited me to walk the Brandon mountain ridge."

"You accepted as I recall," Captain Allen said.

"I should hope you do," Hannah said. "We stopped halfway at Mount Brandon. I slipped and started to fall. You took my hand and pulled me to my feet. Then...you took to that look in your eye."

Captain Allen and Hannah looked away for a moment and then looked down toward the sea.

"I...thought you too forward," Hannah said. "I was not used to losing my wits. Pubs and taverns of winning at billiards and securing the upper hand with people had not prepared me for you."

"We did not finish the full walk," Captain Allen said.

"No. I insisted we turn back," Hannah said. "My employment with the Hardshore estate was so certain, so paramount to my life that I could let no man interfere. I suppose I had Lily to thank for that perception."

"And now?" Captain Allen asked.

Hannah paused.

"You never told me your full name," Hannah said.

"Olaf Allen," he said. "I had planned to tell you when we completed the walk. For at the end is a small monument to my people."

"Olaf is not Irish," Hannah said. "Who are your people?"

"Captain Killian Kent and I grew up together," Captain Allen said. "Our families have lived in Ireland for many generations. He with the red hair, and me with the black. It is no strange thing. I am descended from Vikings of surname 'Olaf'. Proud people celebrating full traditions of the Norse. But as generations stayed in Ireland, they gradually lost those traditions, having been eroded away by Irish customs. Even our surnames changed. From 'Olaf' we became 'Aulay' and then 'Allen'. My first name was given to remind me of my heritage. Tell me, Hannah, what was your impression as we walked along the ridge?"

"Pleasant grassy slopes," Hannah said.

"But only on the western side," Captain Allen said. "The eastern side is dominated by deep corries and sharp cliffs."

"That's right. I did not remember that until now," Hannah said.

"You did not notice at the time, but when you fell, you had done so on the cliff side. You would have perished," Captain Allen said.

"Then the look in your eye was not of self desire," Hannah said. "You...you were truly concerned for my well-being."

"I was both distraught and relieved at what could have been but had not been," Captain Allen said.

"Why didn't you tell me?" Hannah said.

"I could not," he said. "I cared too much to risk hurting you. But you seemed to be hurt as it was. I respected your decision to turn back."

Hannah looked Captain Allen in the eye with deep apology and then smiled.

"I am truly thankful you saved me," she said. "What was it about the cliff side that you said, something about corries."

"Yes," Captain Allen said. "A corrie is a small hollow on the side of a mountain. Sometimes it fills with water and becomes a lake, other times not. There is a myth that a man who falls into a corrie could become trapped. If a lake, he drowns. If not, he goes mad. Yes, mad. He tries to climb his way out but finds no exit. Frustrated, he yells at the mountain to let him pass, and his echo yells at him back. And so he turns his back to the echo, believing that no echo means no mountain blocking his way. He ends up going to the center of the corrie, where an echo greets him from every direction. And no matter which direction he chooses to go, his echo repels him back to center, where he remains until the corrie claims him to dust."

"A Viking should not fear the cliff, the corrie, or the mountain lake," Captain Allen said. "But generation after generation has stripped my family of the Olaf heritage, leaving us as grassy worshippers of name 'Allen'. I wanted to take the ridge alone, many times, to see if I could. But the myth. I was sure to become trapped in a corrie and die. A man can only speak to the mountain for so long before he goes mad. But a man with a companion can survive it. I had hoped to survive it with you."

"When a horse founders, it goes lame," Hannah said. "But you have not gone lame."

"Nor am I a horse!" Captain Allen said.

"I quite agree," Hannah laughed back. "But if you were, I would tell you to change your eats to cure your founder, if any you should have. Pick a different grassy slope. Choose better hay. Dance in a pasture."

"I have never seen a horse dance," Captain Allen said.

"Have you seen two horses dance?" Hannah asked.

Hannah whispered into Captain Allen's ear. The two left the deck at different times and different ways to Captain Allen's cabin. There, Hannah danced for Captain Allen, mimicking what a horse might do. She asked him to try, he at first shied away, but she insisted. Both laughed at his attempts.

And so they danced further. The two then drifted from dancing independently to dancing together.

"Four feet are steadier than two," Hannah said.

"Forty stars of the night twinkle more than four," Captain Allen said.

"Twenty toes and twenty fingers twinkle," Hannah said.

"And dance together under the stars of the sea," Captain Allen said.

"Can the sun catch the moon, if chase should begin?" she said.

"Or the moon chase the sun?" he said.

"Let them chase each other," she said. "He shines by day."

"She shines by night," he said.

"They begin with the Evening Star," she said.

"And continue to the Morning Star," he said.

"Rocked gently by the sea, with the heavens above," she said.

"If the heavens and sea be a corrie, what should I say to the mountains?" Captain Allen said.

"Say nothing. Say nothing more," Hannah said as she leaned into him and pressed her cheek against his.

The evening passed with undulating passion like the soft tickling of a feather upon the rolling waves of the sea. Hannah felt her limbs go numb upon a floating cloud while Captain Allen was drawn by deep desire to Hannah's endearing charm, taking Hannah upon the rolling fields upon horse-drawn chariots of the divine, the horses sending their hooves of delight upon the deep shuddering of the earth.

So overwhelming was this passion that Hannah truly saw herself riding upon such a chariot, with Captain Allen sending the tickle of his whip lightly upon the horses' shoulders. The horses bucked lightly but firmly, sending gentle waves back to the chariot that briefly caused Hannah's vision to swell and shrink, drift and focus, bend yet curve. Hannah's heart thumped in stride with the horses, and they decidedly picked up pace under the firm hand of Captain Allen.

And only just in time. The rolling earth presented a steep upward slope upon a great insurmountable mountain, but the horses took to this slope under Captain Allen's command with renewed strength and speed, commanding their mighty hooves to send the slope below them with the fortitude of no going back. Hannah felt herself being pulled upward in heightened alertness with a mixture of fear, delight, and anticipation of the precipice. There was no stopping the train of passion, and at the very moment where

Hannah felt the chariot carry over the precipice and begin its fall, the horses, chariot, Captain Allen, and she were lifted by a warm updraft of continental strength that carried them through the air and into soft puffy clouds.

The clouds released their charges of energy as Captain Allen and Hannah passed in between. These charges were like lightning in sight but like the buzzing of bees in feel, being subtle in sense but electrifying in deed, lighting up the sky and the two repeatedly, creating auras around the two of varying hues, with pixies of pleasantries dancing about.

Thunderclap after thunderclap shook the two back to their senses. Hannah and Captain Allen found themselves back in his cabin, with soft rain falling upon his ship. The two cuddled and savored their new-found love for each other.

And several more chariot rides.

Chapter 26:

The Cape

On the Confidence, Lily kept herself busy with imaginary sketches of the supposed Africa diamond mine, using her excellent visual skills and years of drawing and design skills. She sketched out fictitious building layouts, machines, and made lists and charts along with business plans relating the "diamond mine" to L M Hardshore Associates. The detail seemed so real that Andre continued to be intrigued by her business and technical skill.

"You might well make an excellent assistant to any architect of war I might hire," he said.

Lily was better than just an "assistant", but Andre had to keep her in her place for his ego's sake. After a time, he assigned her things to design and chart without explaining what they were for.

The Confidence soon approached the Cape of Good Hope. Andre ordered the ship be held back from the port, citing that he would verify Lily's story in case she had spun a trap for him. A longboat was sent to an undeveloped part of the shore.

"Here we wait," Andre said.

The longboat returned shortly, reminding Andre that the Cape was under British rule, and that the last of Dutch claims were ceded to Britain.

"I still have French friends here, from the days France possessed these lands," Andre said.

Andre next insisted that he accompany the next longboat ashore, along with Lily.

"You will not depart my sight for this trip," he said.

Andre and Lily reached shore, and yes, French friends posing as everyday Dutch people met with the two and beckoned them into a secret meeting room. There Andre showed them the documents Lily had produced of the supposed diamond mine. The French allies laughed.

"A deception all along," Andre said. "You will pay for wasting my time."

Lily insisted that they leave at once, but one of the French allies noticed "DeBlanche Consortium" on a document and admitted that yes, while the consortium was based in Ireland, there was a branch of it here, apparently doing mining.

"Half-truths," Andre said.

One of the French allies mentioned that Lily could be playing "Monkey in the Middle" with Andre.

"Just as I close in on a prize, you toss it elsewhere," Andre said to Lily. "We will not leave this Cape until the prize is found. No one will make a monkey out of me!"

Lily was taken to a small holding cell while Andre and his French allies further investigated DeBlanche Consortium activities in the area.

Meanwhile, Lily spent her time staring through a hole in the wall to the outside, barely large enough to fit an apple through. It was her route to the outside, and so she spent time looking, listening, and breathing fresh air from the hole.

In one of the moments she was looking, she was startled to see an eye at the other end.

"Lily," whispered a voice from that person.

"Pierre?" Lily replied, thinking that it sounded like him.

"Yes, it's me," he said, stepping back a bit so she could see him.

"What are you doing here?" she asked.

"No time for that," he said. "Stand aside."

She did, and Pierre tossed a rolled-up document through the hole. It landed on the cell floor as Pierre dashed off.

As Lily knelt down to pick it up, a guard opened the cell door in time to see it. She tried hiding it behind her back, but the guard saw her motion and called for others. They pulled Lily out of the cell and marched her to a meeting room, where Andre and others were discussing their finds after just returning from the DeBlanche Consortium. A guard then pulled the document from Lily and handed it to Andre.

"What is this?" Andre mused, looking over the document.

"I...don't know," Lily said, which was the truth.

"You were searched before you entered the cell and had nothing. Now you have this," Andre said. "Friends on the outside?"

Andre read the document aloud, which instructed Lily to be patient, that her middle namesake would soon have her free.

"Middle namesake," Andre said. "I happen to know that your middle name is 'Marie'. And that your mother had a younger sister named Marie Constance DeBlanche. I also know that Marie is here, at the Cape.

She has been tracked here, after having spent time in Ireland. She is the 'DeBlanche' of DeBlanche Consortium."

"I know nothing of the kind," Lily said, again to gain time.

"Remember this?" Andre said.

> *DeBlanche are so Franch*
> *From Valley are Loire*

"Something you said before," she said.
"Or this?" he said.

> *Lie humbly aside the Shannon Branch tree.*

It seemed that Andre was learning bits of the poem. But twisted. And from where?

"Shall we ask your Aunt Marie?" Andre said.

Lily feigned ignorance, but she couldn't hold it for long. A guard ushered in a woman of 35 years age. Lily recognized the face, though older, as her Aunt Marie Constance DeBlanche. Part of Lily didn't want to believe, the same part that wanted Andre to be a liar.

To say that Lily's mind was swamped with thoughts was no understatement. She tried to resolve things quickly in her mind. Was Lily in a business relationship with Aunt Marie all these years? Somehow it made sense, as they both had an affinity for a realistic view of the world with business and technology. But how was she captured? Perhaps Lily's intuition was too accurate to be fiction—Lily had unfortunately provided Andre with the location of the "overseas mining" location, headed up by Aunt Marie.

Then there was Pierre. How did he get in the Cape? Did he hide on the Confidence all the way down? She was sure he had escaped by longboat to the French mainland. But if he had escaped, what ship did he take to catch up? No other ship in the world could keep up with the Confidence—it was a steamship, after all. The only way would be if...if...

The vane vortex engine must have been adapted for ship use, and Pierre came down on that ship. With Captain Kent.

Lily's heart suddenly lifted such that she felt a dance come upon her. She smiled, laughed, and frolicked around like a little girl at play.

"What is this madness?" Andre asked.

Lady Marie (yes, it was really her) was mortified and wasn't sure what Lily was up to. Such a way to meet a relative after 20-some years!

"Keep away, keep away," Lily said. "Keep me away from the monkeys!"

Andre grabbed her by the arm to arrest her jubilant dance.

"Explain yourself!" he barked.

Lily spoke with mock conceit, saying, "The first man who can find *all* my family fortune may marry me. But hah! I have planted steamboats throughout these shores, from Britain to the Cape, tempting men of all services to come forth and claim me. Do you think the Confidence is the only one of her kind? Nay! She is but the place where I first started this competition, which you believe to be winning. But you are not. Already, there are many such ships on the way. In fact, there is one in the Cape right now! Under your very bristlecone nose!"

"Stop!" Andre said with a slap to her face.

"Marry me then," she said after a moment. "But be sure you lay claim to all my family fortune first, or else there is the clause that it goes elsewhere. My Aunt Marie, for example, has some that even she does not know of. Then there is the third party."

"It's in the poem," Andre said. "I know part of your fortune is in the Loire Valley. And I have disposed of your other 'ships'. This Captain Kent of yours and his ship of sails. That is not the machinatic marvel of the Confidence. I say you are bluffing, Lily, that you are playing me for a monkey in the middle yet again. But it matters not. Lady Marie has first claim on both the diamond mine and the DeBlanche family fortune. I know of the will of Baron DeBlanche. His immediate children come first, grandchildren second. You are second. So it is you, Lily Hardshore of half-British pedigree who is now the monkey in the middle—of nothing."

Lily only grinned.

"Oh, and as another prize, since your purity is no longer necessary, I shall have my way with you—on the night before my wedding to Lady Marie," Andre said with glee.

Lily went from grin to grim.

"Tell him the poem," Lady Marie blurted. "Tell him, and he will spare you."

Lily trembled. This was quite beyond her. She had run out of things to tell. Could she add to the twisted poem? How would she know how much had been told?

"Listen to your aunt, Lily," Andre said.

"I suppose you got part of the poem from her," Lily said to stall for time.

"It was not easy," Andre said. "My French operatives acquired the first two lines from her."

"But you told me that part before we came down here," Lily said.

"To test you," Andre said. "Just another one of my traps."

"The family taught us parts of it," Lily finally "admitted".

"So that no single person could give the entire poem away," Lady Marie added, catching on.

"Three of us were told," Lily said. "We all know the first and last words of each line, to ensure accuracy."

"Say your part, and I will spare you," Andre said.

Lily paused, then said (purposely altering the original):

From April to May,
Then to Main not too far.

French advisers nodded their heads in the affirmative, that the first and last words Lily had just given matched what Lady Marie had previously told them. Obviously Lily and Marie were playing the French people for time. But what of the twisted last line?

"There is one line missing," Andre said. "It is after your line but before the last one."

"He found the last line in the mine," Lady Marie blurted, and for that she received a slap across the face.

Lily understood. Lady Marie had planted that twisted last line for Andre to find. So there was either one last line to find in the mine, or Lily had to come up with one as a decoy for the end. But what end?

"I am convinced that the missing line contains critical details to the French family fortune," Andre said. "We will force them both into the mine until I have it."

"So much for an early marriage," Lily said offhand, hoping to anger Andre.

"I shall put it this way," Andre said sternly. "Whichever of you DeBlanche girls hands over the missing line will marry me and thus be spared. The fate of the other becomes my ever whim until I tire."

That was it. The DeBlanche women were escorted out and toward the diamond mine. Yes, there really was one, as it was Lady Marie who had discovered it. She had a background in geology and had discovered an alluvial vein. But there's no time to recount her history or knowledge. Andre pressed his advantage, and the end was about to unfold.

Chapter 27:

Battle for Blood

The path to the diamond cave was a bit elevated, with a path leading upward from port. The journey took perhaps an hour, but it was reached. Andre, his men, and the DeBlanche women stood at the entrance. Marie and Lily exchanged glances. What was there to say? Lily wondered if she should give Andre the full poem to send him back to France, but that did nothing for preserving her purity. He would still marry Marie and dispose of Lily like refuse.

The day was partly sunny with puffy clouds rolling along. Ocean waves were mild. Fauna flew with flutters of light leisure. The Cape was at complete peace with itself. Lily had a view of the harbor and yes, the Confidence was anchored there.

"In point of fact, I believe both of you know the full poem," Andre said. "I give you one last chance—the first of you to recite that poem will earn a place as my wife. The other will perish. Do I make myself clear?"

A light spray of dust fell on them from the sky, with a taste of salt. It could have been a spray from the ocean, or blown-up dust from afield. However, it did remind Lily of her earlier bluff regarding ships of hers placed all over.

"This is your last chance," Lily returned. "My ships have trained their weapons on you. Give up now, and I will spare your sentence."

Andre laughed. Loudly. He bellowed such a great laugh that it carried into the mountain and echoed back outward toward port with such reverberation as to sound fully demonic and pitiless. More salt dust fell, and it caused much irritation to the fair skins of Lily and Marie. They attempted to wrench free and flee, and they actually did momentarily, but French guards walled them off a bit away from the cave entrance and gradually forced them back.

Without warning, a sound of hot-sizzling intensity approached rapidly from overhead. Landing between the DeBlanche women and the cave entrance, a massive salt cannon ball shattered upon impact, startling everyone there.

Some shouted that the mountain was falling, others that the sky was falling, but Lily noticed a nearly-obscured ship slowly approaching the harbor. From that ship left periodic puffs of smoke. It wasn't the Confidence, but it was another ship with the ability to harness steam.

More rounds came, causing mass confusion. Lily exchanged glances with Marie and pointed at the ship. Marie understood, but before they could decide where to go, French soldiers approached the cave's entrance from inside.

Several salt cannon balls landed on the cave entrance, causing its collapse. Several others landed on the upward slope of the cave entrance, causing a blocked inner mountain stream to let forth and pour outward. It filled the collapsed bits of the cave entrance, found a weakness, and then pushed downward into the cave, flooding it and any French who had survived the initial collapse.

The resulting flood carried those outside the cave entrance downward toward the port. The Confidence, still controlled by Andre's allies, had by now been equipped for attack, and it fired upon the mystery ship, which continued to play hide-and-seek with the Confidence. However, it sent salt cannon balls atop the Confidence, scaring the crew if nothing else, but in fact only minor damage came about.

The flood of water had turned into a mudslide. As it reached the bottom of the slope, two sets of British soldiers flooded in from each side, with Captain Kent leading one group. It was too close for muskets, and so the groups fought sword-to-sword.

Andre stuck close to the DeBlanche women, who could not yet get away. Captain Kent made gains toward Andre, and when the two received sight of each other, Andre stabbed Marie and used the diversion to flee with Lily, returning a big grin and a bellow that once again he had taken Captain Kent's prize.

With Marie injured and badly bleeding, Captain Kent (who was divided by the spilled blood), tended to Marie and stopped the bleeding with a rip of his own shirt. Soon the British had enough control of the skirmish to help Marie, who urged Captain Kent to go after Andre to free Lily.

Andre signaled to the Confidence, which in turn let out a fog of steam for cover. He then took a longboat out to the Confidence with Lily as his captive. Once aboard, the Confidence took to maneuvers to destroy the mystery ship attacking it.

The mystery ship, in turn, let out a fog of steam itself. It moved to a pre-agreed location where Captain Kent boarded. The ship, as may be guessed, was Lady Jack Nine. Pierre had been ordering the salt cannon shots while Captain Kent had led the land attack. Salt cannon balls were made from separating salt from the ocean water when refeeding the boiler with fresh water.

No time for that now. The two ships exchanged rounds and fog, and rounds and fog. Only light damage accumulated, and the only thing wearing thin was nerves. Captain Kent was beside himself each minute that passed, and he tried all sorts of maneuvers to corner off the Confidence, but with the poor visibility, it was more of a stalemate.

"This must end," Captain Kent said. "I cannot bear the thought of Lily in danger any longer."

"We need a larger explosive," Pierre said.

"Yes, we do," Captain Kent replied with a sudden thought. "Pierre. Give me an hour to get Lily off that ship."

"And then?" Pierre asked.

"Set Lady Jack Nine to intercept and destroy the Confidence. With an explosion," Captain Kent said.

"But we have no explosive big enough to destroy the Confidence," Pierre said.

"Ah but we do. The vane vortex engine," Captain Kent said. "Set it and the boiler to self-destruct on impact."

"You will be killed, along with Lily," Pierre said.

"She is dead already if I don't rescue her," Captain Kent said. "And so am I."

Pierre reluctantly agreed. Captain Kent took a small boat through the fog toward where he thought the Confidence was. He could only use his sense of hearing for such a location reference, from the firing of rounds from time to time. However, just as Captain Kent approached what he thought was the location, the firing stopped. He could hear nothing.

Then, like the whistling of a tea kettle, he heard a sound. In fact, it would soon go past him! Reaching out with both hands, he grabbed hold onto a trailing rope of the Confidence and pulled himself aboard. Fog from the steam engine was still being released, and so he had cover from the French crew.

Pierre had previously instructed Captain Kent on the layout of the Confidence, and so Captain Kent knew where he eventually had to go, the upper observation deck. But first came the setup. Through stealthy measures, he crept along until he reached the boiler room. After quietly strangling several men, he adjusted the controls so that the boiler would explode upon contact.

Captain Kent then made his way through the ship until he reached the observation deck. The fog cleared, and there with Andre was Lily.

"Let her go," Captain Kent ordered.

French guards rushed to the observation deck on hearing Captain Kent, but Andre only permitted two up—to hold Lily while Andre engaged in sword play with Captain Kent. Except there was nothing playful about it.

The two went at it, and again it was nearly stalemate, though Andre did get in a few swipes that cut through Captain Kent's clothing and drew blood from his arm. With blood pouring down to his hand, Kent's grip slipped, and his sword fell. Now desperate to defend himself, he used anything and everything available, throwing various things at Andre.

Andre laughed, as did the French men holding Lily.

"You are hardly a challenge like this, Captain Kent!" Andre said.

"Give up, Andre," Captain Kent said.

"You have a weak heart for the weak," Andre said, referring to Lily.

The group heard a distant wispy whistle, like that of a yet-to-be-invented jet engine.

"Check on the boiler," Andre said to the French men as they tossed Lily back to him to go below.

As Lily was tossed to Andre, part of her garment ripped, revealing a hidden document. While Andre held Captain Kent at bay by sword, Andre took the document and read part of it.

DeBlanche are so Franch
From Valley are Loire

"The entire poem is here," Andre said to Lily. "You lied!"

Andre tossed Lily overboard. She screamed all the way down into the water. Shocked, Captain Kent started for Andre, but Andre pressed the tip of his sword.

"The DeBlanche family fortune, in my hand!" Andre bragged. "This is what every man wants. And you can't have it!"

The wispy whistle grew uncomfortably loud. Captain Kent twisted and jumped off the observation deck in the direction of Lily, falling to an unknown future. His last sight was of Andre leaning over the side toward Captain Kent, gloating in triumph with the document in hand.

Lady Jack Nine collided with the Confidence. The resulting explosion sent shockwaves throughout the Cape. Captain Kent was momentarily stunned, but after several seconds, he regained his senses only to be subjected to raining debris. Where Lily was, he could not tell, but he called and swam about in hopes of finding her.

As it was, the flying debris coincided with a passing storm cloud. Winds picked up, and it began to rain. Waves grew taller and forced Captain Kent against the rocks. Whereas any other man would have pulled himself up the rocks to safety, Captain Kent swam around in hopes of finding Lily. As luck would have it, he saw her floating face-down in the water just a little around a rock cluster. Swimming around the cluster (and getting beat up by wave and rock in the process), he managed to grab hold of her and pull her up from the wave and rock and thus to safety.

Rain poured down. Captain Kent held tightly onto Lily, who started to cough up water and regain her breath.

"You are safe," he said. "I will not let you go."

Chapter 28:

A Farewell Return

In the aftermath, British forces went through the Cape and cleaned up. Remaining French forces were rounded up and imprisoned. The French crew on the Confidence were found and declared dead. Andre, though presumed to be dead with them, was never fully identified. Many such dead from the Confidence could not be.

Pierre and crew of Lady Jack Nine had escaped in longboats before sending the ship at the Confidence. Yes, the wispy whistling sound was that of the vane vortex engine on full overload on a collision course for the Confidence.

Captain Kent and Lily were rescued from the rocks and taken to proper rest facilities on the Cape. With their rescue, full peace of the region was established.

The diamond mine was never found, despite futile attempts to rediscover its entrance. The mountain face had too badly contorted itself to obscure its location, and so all efforts were given up.

Lady Marie Constance was attended to by a doctor and was patched up. Though weak from blood loss, she recovered day by day, as did Captain Kent's wound and Lily's nerves.

In the time that followed, the Pearl of the Sea arrived with Captain Allen and Hannah in shock as to the debris still present in the area. Both Lady Jack Nine and the Confidence made for a prominent display near the harbor, enough of one that no other ship was at risk of running aground it while giving dire warning of what could happen to colliding ships.

Pierre was granted his freedom and British citizenry by the Royal Crown. A special celebration was held afterward, the first celebration where Lady Marie was well enough to get around.

It was time to return. Captain Allen gave orders for his crew to assist the others to take quarter on Pearl of the Sea as his guests. These guests included Captain Kent, Lily, and Marie Constance.

Pierre and the Lady Jack Nine crew stayed behind at the Cape in hopes of resurrecting Lady Jack Nine. Captain Kent admitted that this would be a formidable task, but Pierre said that now he had his own freedom, it was time to repay his good fortune by granting Lady Jack Nine her own freedom. Captain Kent laughed.

The journey back was leisurely and uneventful, taking Pearl of the Sea all the way back to England. Lord M had hardly noticed Lily was gone at all, wondering if she had taken a time of leisure in London or somewhere near the sea. Seeing Hannah's unopened letter to him on his desk that should have advised of her kidnapping, and to keep things short, Lily admitted that yes, she had spent time near the sea.

All had recovered. The best news of all came, that Napoleon was defeated at Waterloo. With that, the Napoleonic Wars came to an end.

The overseas mining had come to an end for DeBlanche Consortium. Lady Marie thanked Lily for putting her up in London for continued recovery, but it was time for Lady Marie to return to Ireland and continue her business there, so that DeBlanche Consortium and L M Hardshore Associates could continue to help people have a better life.

One bit of a surprise, however, was that Captain Allen and Hannah announced both their engagement and wedding, to be held in Ireland itself. Lily, Captain Kent, Lady Marie, and many others were invited. The other Hardshores were invited, but Lord M and Lord M's mother were too content with the Hardshore estate and declined. Also not there was Pierre, who was still at the Cape. Lily felt sad that Pierre, who had helped her so much, could not attend, but Captain Kent reminded Lily that this was Hannah's day, and so to be happy for her.

The wedding went well. Captain Kent was the best man while Lily was the maid of honor. Lady Marie along with several others were bridesmaids. The reception was jubilantly filled with food, drink, music, and general merriment. Hannah and Captain Allen showed off their new home in Ireland, a large estate with plenty of friendly animals. Happily settled into her new life, Hannah bade farewell to her invited guests, extending perpetual invitations to all.

The topic of Lady Marie's childhood came up, and so Lady Marie showed Lily and Captain Kent where she grew up at a nunnery there in Ireland. The nuns were more than happy to see Lady Marie, even bragging that they brought her up "right" so that she would succeed in the world. The nuns showed where Lady

Marie had stayed, in a little house where several other orphans had been raised. In one small storage room were saved sentimental items that Lady Marie had made for the nuns over the years, including school notes on her studies for geology, mining, coal, steam power, and business.

One other thing in storage was the poem:

> *DeBlanche are so Franch*
> *From Valley are Loire*
> *From Main we go May*
> *Then to April not too far.*
> *A rock, a stone, a Shannon Blank tree*
> *Lie hum-bl-y aside the grotto number three.*

There were also detailed notes about the poem, such as the meaning of "Main", "May", and "April".

"These notes tell exactly where the family fortune is," Lily said.

"I figured it out after much study with the nuns," Lady Marie said.

"You could have told Andre, to spare your life," Lily said.

"But I didn't," Lady Marie said with a smile. "As long as France was in turmoil, there was no point in going back. I had hoped for this day when peace would come of France. Perhaps the peace will hold out."

"Perhaps it will," Lily said.

"I used to have wonderful aspirations as to what kind of treasure our family has in store," Lady Marie said. "But now I find that here in Ireland with my business is my great treasure. The venture in Africa was risky and too far from home. I see that now. I will not travel so far away again."

Lady Marie handed her poem notes to Lily.

"I give you charge of the family fortune, to find it and do great things with it," Lady Marie said.

"It is part yours too," Lily said.

"Then my Lily Marie Hardshore, I take it that you intend to continue doing business with me," Lady Marie said with a smile.

The two hugged and bade each other farewell.

Chapter 29:

DeßBlanche so Franch

Lily and Captain Kent took to a French journey from England by ship to find the DeBlanche family fortune. After a bit of travel, they landed in Saint-Nazaire and took a coach eastward along the Loire River much as Lord M had first done many years before. The landscape was not as beautiful as it was before, having been ravaged by war, but the people were welcoming, especially since Lily spoke French as well as anyone.

> *DeBlanche are so Franch*
> *From Valley are Loire*
> *From Main we go May*
> *Then to April not too far.*
> *A rock, a stone, a Shannon Blank tree*
> *Lie hum-bl-y aside the grotto number three.*

From Lady Marie's notes, the two followed the Loire River until they reached "Main" or the Maine River. There they stayed the night at an inn to contemplate the next step.

By morning, it was time to resume the trip.

> *From Main we go May*

The two followed the Maine River until they reached the Mayenne River.

Then to April not too far.

The two continued just past Avrillé, but not too far.

"My father's old vineyard," Lily exclaimed. "I can see it from here. My mother once showed it to me when I was but four years old. It seems so small now, but it's overgrown. There are no grape vines anywhere. I remember there used to be a guesthouse. Let's go see."

The guesthouse had long ago been razed, with all evidence of its former location removed. The area where it once stood was fully overgrown and devoid of anything Lord M had seen in his last visit.

The question became this—was the DeBlanche family fortune hidden somewhere on the old Hardshore vineyard property? Lily also remembered that there was a DeBlanche chateau, but having only the memory of a four-year old, she couldn't remember where.

"We must look for a rock, a stone, and a Shannon Blank tree," Lily said.

"I've never heard of a Shannon Blank tree," Captain Kent said. "Very strange name."

"Yes, it is," Lily agreed. "Unless...these names in the poem are English forms of French names. 'Main' becomes 'Maine River', 'May' becomes 'Mayenne', 'April' becomes 'Avrillé'.

"Rock and stone seem English enough," Captain Kent said.

"But as you pointed out, 'Shannon Blank' tree is not," Lily said. "There must be a French-sounding name for that."

It was a puzzle that eluded Lily.

"I think I know the answer," Captain Kent said. "And I can see why you have not solved it. Your father has spent his life in the care of plants."

"True," Lily acknowledged.

"But you have not," Captain Kent said.

"Also true," Lily said.

"We stand here in a vineyard, where French grapes were grown," Captain Kent said.

"But none are here now," Lily said. "If there were, they might give a clue."

"This 'Shannon Blank' is 'Chenin Blanc', a white wine," Captain Kent said.

Lily looked around the old vineyard. The two walked around as she searched for a Chenin Blanc vine. There was none.

"No Chenin Blanc vine, not even a grotto," Lily mused. "There's nothing here."

Lily sat on a large rock to rest.

"You're sitting on a rock," Captain Kent said.

"Just a rock," she said. "Could it be part of the poem? I see nothing else around."

In fact, the rock was by an overgrown embankment. Lily stood up and backed up as if getting a better view of what might be around the rock. Captain Kent took out his sword and slashed through the overgrowth to reveal a tunnel by the rock.

"This isn't a stone," Captain Kent said.

"But it is a stone tunnel," Lily said. "Come. We must find the other end."

The two followed the same tunnel Lord M had followed years earlier. On reaching its exit, Lily was horrified to see that the old DeBlanche chateau was in ruins. Tears rolled down her cheeks as she felt a part of her family had perished over a petty war. Captain Kent consoled her, but at length, she proceeded to look around for other clues. She didn't see any.

"This is just as overgrown as the other side," Captain Kent said, pulling out his sword to slash through the overgrowth.

"Wait," Lily said as she suddenly saw something. "Do not yet slash what might be fruitful."

Lily saw two small grapes clinging to a spindly vine, barely clinging to life as it seemed to drown under the onslaught of overgrowth. The two looked closer at the vine.

"Is it?" she asked.

"Yes," he said.

The two realized that a particularly large amount of overgrowth was actually shrouding a stone structure.

"Allow me," Lily said, who gently pulled the growth aside to reveal the entrance to this structure.

Carved into the stonework by the entrance were three grape leaves of lobes five, three, and three.

"Three leaves," Captain Kent said.

"Grotto number three," Lily replied. "Is it here?"

The grotto was dark until their eyes adjusted, and then the two realized there was a source of light. A fountain had glowing algae on the bottom and inner sides. They gave soft undulations of light of slowly shifting colors. One particular ornament was a cup holder with a cup still in it. Lily removed the cup to dip it into the water, which she did, and she then handed it to Captain Kent for him to drink.

"Thank you," he said.

She looked for another cup to drink from, but she could find none. Thinking it odd, she half-fancied a cup magically appearing as she put her hand on the cup holder. The two heard a click, and a secret door opened, revealing a treasure.

"The DeBlanche family fortune!" Lily exclaimed. "Look, there's a note."

Lily read the note, and she cried. She handed it to Captain Kent.

"It is written to whoever might find it," Captain Kent said, "That Lord M Hardshore was here and danced with a beautiful woman in his arms, Lady Antoinette DeBlanche. May whoever of her kin find this remember her as the most gracious and loving woman in France."

"My father never told me any of this," Lily said. "How he could have spared me much. He should have told me straight away. Things would be different."

"They would be," Captain Kent said. "You would be different and in a different place. We never would have met. And that would be the greatest loss of treasure above all."

Captain Kent dropped to a knee and spoke:

"Lily Hardshore, will you marry me?"

Lily placed her hands over her mouth in shock. She had vowed that no man would marry her for her fortune. But there Captain Kent was, by the family fortune proposing to her.

"I can't allow any man to claim my fortune," she hesitated.

"You are the only fortune I see here," he said.

Lily clasped his hands and lifted him to his feet.

"Yes," she said with a hug and kiss.

The two embraced for a further moment.

"You do know that L M Hardshore will continue with me at the helm," she said. "I cannot allow others to run it."

"I understand," he said.

"And the DeBlanche family fortune will be used for good deeds here in France, without others intervening," she continued.

"I understand that too," he said. "I only want you."

The two embraced and kissed again.

Lily did as she said. She established a business presence in France, using the family fortune. The DeBlanche chateau was rebuilt into a school for girls to learn business and even included a study of vineyards and grapes.

Once all business ventures were secured in L M Hardshore Associates, Lily made plans for the wedding, to be held at the mouth of the Loire River in Saint-Nazaire.

The wedding was beautiful. Lady Marie was the maid of honor with Captain Allen the best man. Hannah was a bridesmaid. Lord M showed up and was overly eager to give his daughter away.

The guest list was long, very long, and soon the group settled into an ocean-side reception filled with food and wine. As stomachs filled and moods became light, music started up as did much dancing. Dusk came around; the evening started into the night.

But just before the dusk completely faded, fireworks danced in the night sky from a ship in the harbor. It was an unexpected surprise, as Lily with her business sense had planned everything. As the wedding party and guests enjoyed the fireworks, Lily had to know from where they came. She rushed up to a pier just as the fireworks completed and watched as a ship approached.

"Hello!" said a familiar voice.

"Pierre!" Lily called back.

"What a pleasant surprise!" Captain Kent said.

But as the ship docked, Captain Kent gained a sense of familiarity.

"Lady Jack Nine!" Captain Kent shouted.

Pierre walked from the ship to the pier.

"I salvaged her and restored her masts," Pierre said. "She's not as fast as when she had the vane vortex engine, but she *is* a Baltimore clipper. That's plenty fast for me. Isn't she beautiful?"

"I have my own beauty right here," Captain Kent said, giving Lily a hug and a smooch.

Pierre smiled.

"Well don't just stand there," Lily finally said. "Come join us for the party."

Pierre did. And it was said to be the most wonderful celebration of matrimony ever.

Somewhere on the high seas of the world, a fishing net pulled in a bedraggled man, who had been drifting for uncounted time. The fishermen, not sure if this skeleton of a man be alive or dead, took him aboard and freed him of the net. They gave him spirits and asked him his name.

"Andre DeVille," he said.

The End